BEHR'S REBEL
FEATURING THE PREQUEL RAIA'S PETS

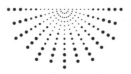

S.E. SMITH

ACKNOWLEDGMENTS

I would like to thank my husband Steve for believing in me and being proud enough of me to give me the courage to follow my dream. I would also like to give a special thank you to my sister and best friend, Linda, who not only encouraged me to write, but who also read the manuscript. Also, to my other friends who believe in me: Julie, Jackie, Christel, Sally, Jolanda, Lisa, Laurelle, Debbie, and Narelle. The girls that keep me going!

And a special thanks to Paul Heitsch, David Brenin, Samantha Cook, Suzanne Elise Freeman, and PJ Ochlan—the awesome voices behind my audiobooks!

—S.E. Smith

Behr's Rebel
featuring the prequel Raia's Pets
Copyright © 2021 by Susan E. Smith
First E-Book Published October 2021
Cover Design by S.E. Smith

ALL RIGHTS RESERVED: This literary work may not be reproduced or transmitted in any form or by any means, including electronic or photographic reproduction, in whole or in part, without express written permission of the author.

All characters, places, and events in this book are fictitious or have been used fictitiously, and are not to be construed as real. Any resemblance to actual persons living or dead, actual events, locales or organizations are strictly coincidental.

Summary: Raia's Pets: An orphaned human girl living in an alien world befriends two adorable pets with very unusual powers.

Summary: Behr's Rebel: A dangerous commission to rescue an imprisoned rebel leader entangles a skillful freighter pilot and her two powerful pets in a fight against the might of the Marastin Dow military.

ISBN: 978-1-956052-21-3 (ebook)
ISBN: 978-1-956052-22-0 (paperback)

{1. Romance—Fiction. 2. Science Fiction Romance—Fiction. 3. Paranormal Romance—Fiction. 4. Short Story—Fiction.—5. Fantasy}

Published by Montana Publishing, LLC
& SE Smith of Florida Inc. www.sesmithfl.com

CONTENTS

RAIA'S PETS

Chapter 1	7
Chapter 2	18
Chapter 3	26
Chapter 4	34
Chapter 5	40
Chapter 6	49

BEHR'S REBEL

Chapter 1	61
Chapter 2	71
Chapter 3	83
Chapter 4	91
Chapter 5	100
Chapter 6	109
Chapter 7	117
Chapter 8	125
Chapter 9	136
Chapter 10	146
Chapter 11	156
Chapter 12	165
Chapter 13	177
Chapter 14	187
Chapter 15	195
Epilogue	207
Note from the Author	212
Additional Books	213
About the Author	217

RAIA'S PETS

CAST OF CHARACTERS

Marastin Dow:

Behr De'Mar: Leader of the Marastin Dow Rebellion

Evetta Marquette: Former Marastin Dow Engineer Technician First Class

Hanine Marquette: Former Marastin Dow Engineering Programmer Third Class

Inez Reddick: Marastin Dow medic murdered by Kejon Hands

General Mieka Reddick

General Marus Tylis

Captain Taylah Marks

Berman De'Mar: Scientist and father to Behr

Nayua Cooper: Young daughter of Hanine and Aaron

Marastin Dow warships:

Traitor's Run: Commanded by Captain Tylis

Nebula One: Commanded by General Behr De'Mar

Humans:

Raia Glossman: Short-haul trader captain, explorer, and trader of rare antiquities.

Ben Cooper: mated to **Evetta Marquette**; living on Curizan home world of Ceran-Pax.

Aaron Cooper: mated to **Hanine Marquette**; living on Curizan home world of Ceran-Pax.

Curizan:

General Razdar Bahadur: Spy and Commander of an elite division of Curizan Special Forces.

Ha'ven Ha'darra: Prince and leader of the Curizan

Adalard Ha'darra: Prince and brother of Ha'ven and twin brother of Jazen Ha'darra

Jazen 'Arrow' Ha'darra: Prince and brother of Ha'ven and twin brother of Adalard Ha'darra

Kejon Hands: Traitor and mercenary trying to overthrow the Curizan, Valdier, and Sarafin royal families.

Captain K'lard Astar: Captain of the Curizan Escort Ship *Challenger*

Zebulon: Valdier dragon-shifter; Prince Mandra Reykill's Chief Security Officer

Alien Species:

Ander Ray: Tearnat; a large blue-green reptilian species known for their fierceness, agility, and stealth.

Chummy: A small, black and white spotted Quazin Chumloo. Quazin Chumloos are endangered. They are extremely intelligent with telepathic, psychoscopy, and levitative abilities.

Pi: A tan and white Marica Peekaboo. Thought to be extremely rare. Marica Peekaboos possess telekinetic, precognitive, and apportational abilities, making the exact numbers of Marica Peekaboos in existence difficult to calculate.

Glub: Gelation Shopkeeper on Sanapare

Willia: Glub's wife and Shopkeeper owner on Sanapare

Frope: Tiliqua shopkeeper on Sanapare

Orb: Hoggian assassin from the Keltar regions

He'lo: a Triloug assassin

Akita Maradash: Enhanced Marastin Dow assassin and sister to General Reynar Maradash

Spaceports:

Yardell: located on the far side of Curizan star system

Kardosa: Large spaceport known for its robust trading

Sanapare: Lavish spaceport frequented by the wealthy

Language:

Trinorsis helo! Traitor's hell!

Chimaigchi tie mol lot. You speak Chimaigchi.

Non-sentient Species:

Rougeworms: disgusting subterranean creatures with no eyes and large round mouths filled with teeth that devour everything in their path.

RAIA'S SYNOPSIS

Friends from other worlds...

Although Raia Glossman is human, she only remembers one world—the alien one where she was raised by her Tearnat Guardian, Ander Rays. Her love for exploration and new discoveries comes from Ander.

While on a quest to find the perfect birthday gift, she instead finds two very unusual, and powerful, furry friends. Now all she has to do is explain to her Tearnat guardian why they should be allowed to stay despite his 'no pets' policy!

Chummy, a Quazin Chumloo, is a rare species with powerful abilities that few know about. Captured by poachers, he is rescued from certain death by the inquisitive and equally talented Pi. Unfortunately, not even Pi has the ability to completely free him.

Pi, a Marica Peekaboo, loves the marketplace. It is a treasure trove of goodies to eat and wonderful shiny objects to steal. With each new arrival, she finds something unique to add to her hidden collection of stolen goods—including Chummy and a strange alien girl named Raia.

Three very different worlds collide, and freedom for an entire species is at stake. Can a friendship forged in a back alley be powerful enough to survive an immense alien universe where danger lurks at every turn?

CHAPTER ONE

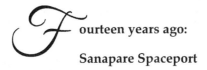 ourteen years ago:

Sanapare Spaceport

"Raia, don't go far. We won't be here long," Ander Ray cautioned in his deep, gritty voice.

"I won't," Raia replied.

Ander shook his head as he watched his strange ward disappear into the crowd. He would probably end up spending half of his time at the Spaceport chasing after her. He winced when the merchant he had come to visit slapped him on the shoulder with a beefy hand.

"You know, if you ever wanted to sell her, I could probably get you a large sum of credits in exchange," Glub casually mentioned.

Ander pulled back his thick lips to reveal rows of sharp white teeth. A shudder ran through Glub's gelatinous green body.

"Raia is off limits," he snapped.

"Of course, Ander. I meant no offense. I know how much that girl means to you. It was a poor joke," Glub hastily replied.

"Do you have the items I requested?" Ander demanded.

"Yes, in the back. Have a seat, I will bring them to you," Glub hurriedly answered.

Ander looked over his shoulder, hoping Raia would be somewhere in sight. As usual, she wasn't. He pulled a small metal tracking device from his waistcoat, flipped the top open, and pinpointed Raia's location. She was at the Odds and Ends store five buildings down.

"Would you like a nice cup of tea, Captain?" Glub's mate inquired politely, her voice soft and feminine.

He nodded. "Yes, please, Willia. Do you have any Mythroot?" he asked.

"Of course. I keep some here for your visits. Is Raia with you this trip?" Willia responded, looking around the shop.

He chuckled and nodded. "Yes, but she is off exploring," he replied.

"I hope she stops by. I have some fresh Buttersweets that she might enjoy," Willia said, placing a tray with the cup of hot tea and the tea kettle on a small, antique table with two chairs on either side of it.

"I'll let her know," he replied, tucking his long blue-green tail aside and sitting down.

He placed his dark brown, wide-brimmed hat in the other chair and set the tracking device on the table, idling stroking the casing. Raia was on the move again.

Ander picked up the cup of steaming tea. The fragrance of the thick, creamy brew teased his senses, causing the thin slits of his nostrils to open and close rapidly as he inhaled the delicious scent. He flicked out his long tongue and almost groaned aloud with pleasure as the first sip of tea slid down his throat.

He sat back in the chair and absently studied the pedestrians walking along the sidewalk outside of the antiquities shop. His mind drifted to

Raia, and he traced the fragile cup with the tip of his sharp claw as he mulled over how fast Raia was growing up.

At fourteen, she was beginning to… develop in ways that were going to make his life very interesting in the next few years. He lifted a hand and ran his claws along his ridged brow. It was hard to believe that Raia had only been with him for ten years.

"Here are the items you requested, Ander," Glub announced.

Ander blinked, nodded, and motioned for Glub to place the box on the table. He moved aside the fine porcelain tea cup and kettle so that Glub's gelatinous body wouldn't accidentally knock it off the table. It was ironic that such a large man owned a shop filled with delicate treasures.

He opened the box as soon as Glub slid back several feet and carefully examined the objects inside. All the items he had requested were there, plus one more that he hadn't. After a moment, Ander withdrew a bag of credits from his coat and tossed it to Glub.

Glub caught the bag and shimmered with delight. "Is there anything else you are looking for?" he eagerly inquired.

"Perhaps some wrapping for a gift," Ander requested.

"Of course, I have some in the back," Glub said.

"Take your time. I would like to enjoy my tea while it is still hot," Ander replied.

"No hurry. I'm sure Raia would enjoy more time to explore," Glub chuckled.

Ander nodded and waited until Glub moved away before he reached for the silk wrapped item inside the box that he had not asked for. He carefully removed a small, cheap glass sculpture of a Tasier from the cloth wrapping.

He frowned as he turned the sculpture over in his hand. He rubbed an odd etching along one leg with the edge of his thumb. Looking up, he scanned the area outside of the store. Nothing suspicious stood out.

He glided the pad of his thumb over the spot again. Dipping the tip of his finger in his tea, he coated the imprints with the liquid and revealed a series of markings that he hadn't seen in years. Two encrypted words appeared.

Keep safe.

There was only one person who had ever communicated with him in this way—Berman De'Mar. A fellow scientist with the same passion for history that he had. He had lost touch with Berman nearly ten years ago.

He was curious as to why Berman would contact him now after such a long absence. He was even more curious about why a man with such a great passion for antiquities would be sending him a cheap tourist bauble. Checking again to make sure he wasn't observed, he lifted the glass sculpture and hit the top of it against the corner of the metal table.

The head of the Tasier snapped off. Holding the figurine over the palm of his hand, he turned it upside down and caught the intricate crystal disk and small folded message hidden inside. Memories flooded him —along with a growing sense of urgency to depart. He quickly slid the disk in the spine of a book he had bought for Raia.

"Here you go, my friend," Glub announced. "Willia found some colorful paper for Raia's gift."

Ander quickly rewrapped the broken figurine in the silk, returned it to its place beside the other items, and resealed the box before he reached for the paper Glub had placed on the table.

A commotion sounded outside, and Glub chuckled. "You may want to hurry. I believe your Raia has found herself some trouble."

Ander glanced at the crowd and grimly nodded. "I fear you may be right. Please thank Willia for the tea," he said as he gathered up the book and the box.

"Come back again!" Glub called after him.

Raia worried her bottom lip as she studied all the items on the shelf in the curiosity shop. She was looking for something special. After all, today was her birthday, and she would never be this age again. Well, she would be for a whole year, but *today* was super special because it was the first day of that year.

She clutched the small bag of credits that Ander had given her right before they disembarked from their ship. There were so many cool shops filled with all kinds of really awesome things to buy that she didn't know where to start. Just when she thought she found one thing she wanted, something else would catch her eye.

"Hey, we don't allow pets in here," the shopkeeper growled in annoyance.

Raia scanned the room, searching for the cause of the shopkeeper's irritation. Her eyes widened when she realized he was glaring accusingly at her. She lifted her hand and pointed a finger at her chest.

"Are you talking to me?" she inquired with raised eyebrows.

The two-headed Tiliqua gave her a sharp nod with both heads. "Who else would I be talking to? Hey! What are you doing? You a thief?" the other head barked.

Raia opened her mouth to retort that she had credits when she saw a flash of sparkles out of the corner of her eye. She uttered a startled squeak when a ball of tan and white fur rolled across her feet and shot out the door. She gaped in awe when the creature unfurled and grinned at her with large, luminous eyes before taking off on four legs.

"You owe me for that!" the shopkeeper yelled.

Raia looked back and forth in disbelief at the Tiliqua and the spot where the creature had just been. The shopkeeper scurried around the counter with a large pole in his hands, and she backed up instinctively, bumping into a small table. The backpack she was wearing knocked over several items and they fell to the floor with a sickening crash. She twisted around and hurriedly straightened the few items she hadn't knocked off the shelf while she kept an eye on the furious merchant.

"That creature wasn't mine. I don't have any pets," she defended, scrambling to untangle her backpack from the scarves caught on the zipper.

"I saw you two come in together. You better have credits for the items that beast stole and those you broke!" the shopkeeper shouted.

Raia winced when she swung around and her arm knocked a dozen small black containers to the floor. Dozens of small black crab-like creatures poured from the boxes, their large double pincers snapping furiously at her boots. A squeak of alarm slipped from her as she hopped and twisted to get away from them.

"I'll have you arrested for destroying my store! Security! Security! Thief!! I have a thief!" the Tiliqua roared from both of his mouths.

"I'm s-sorry. I'm sorry," Raia said before she twirled and fled from the shop.

She turned to the left, cringing when she heard the yelps of the shopkeeper and the sound of crashing behind her. Searching wildly for a place to hide, she noticed two security officers heading her way.

She pulled in a shaking breath and darted behind a large stack of woven baskets. After waiting for the two guards to pass by, she threaded her way through the alley between the two shops. Once she was certain they couldn't see her, she took off at a rapid pace through the crowded market.

She was nearly ten stores away when one of the guards behind her yelled loudly. Glancing over her shoulder, she cringed when the two security guards pushed through the crowd, heading in her direction. Panic coursed through her, and she took off, sprinting through the crowd while desperately searching for a place to hide. She spotted a wide structural beam and slipped within the contours of the h-shaped beam. Seconds later, the heavy pounding of booted feet slowed and paused on the other side of the beam.

Holding her breath, Raia pulled her backpack around to her chest and pressed her back against the massive metal beam. She focused on slowing her breathing and remained motionless. She leaned her head back and waited.

"Let's just write this up. This is the third time this week that Frope has accused someone of bringing a pet into his shop and stealing from him," one of the guards breathlessly groaned.

"Do you think it was the same creature that was seen down on Level 2?" the other guard asked.

"Sounds like it to me. I'll ask Command to send a trapper for it. It probably came in off one of the ships…."

Raia breathed a sigh of relief when the guards' voices faded as they walked away. The sound of metal-against-metal came to her from the alley. She tightened her arms around her backpack. The narrow section was a service passage. It was barely wide enough for her to fit in.

Gnawing on her bottom lip, she peered around the beam. She could see the two security personnel still standing across from the shops. She took a deep breath, pulled her backpack back on, and stuffed the small bag of credits into the inner pocket of her dark brown jacket.

"Well, you wanted to have an exciting birthday," she muttered.

Gripping the straps of her backpack, she slowly began walking down the alley. She kept reminding herself that this spaceport wasn't like the others that she and Ander usually visited. This one was more upscale. There were no monsters hiding in the dark alley, waiting to slit the throats of an unwary visitor.

At least I hope there aren't, she silently prayed.

Her footsteps faltered when the sound of metal-on-metal rang through the alley again. It sounded like someone was banging on something— like they were trying to open a metal door or grate. She cautiously peered behind a large electrical box. Reaching into her pocket, she pulled out a small light and turned it on. The banging stopped, and a pair of luminous eyes peered up at her out of the darkness.

"It's you!" she quietly hissed, staring down at the bundle of tan and white fur.

The fur ball had been banging on a heavy metal lock that held a small cage closed. Pieces of partially eaten fruit lay scattered around the cage with a variety of other items. The bars were scraped and chipped, and broken pieces of metal lay on the ground, testaments to previous failed attempts to open the cage.

"Hey, do you need some help?" Raia gently asked.

She slowly stepped around the electrical box, holding her free hand out. The fur ball climbed on top of the cage and carefully studied her. She giggled when it smiled at her and held out a partially eaten piece of fruit. She shook her head.

"No, thank you. I've already eaten," she murmured.

A muffled sniff drew her attention back to the cage. She carefully shrugged off her backpack and knelt. Peering inside the cage, she noticed an adorable creature with large, round eyes, black and white spotted fur, huge rounded ears, tiny paws, and a long fluffy tail. The white, fluffy fur that ran under its chin and down along its chest was filthy. Her heart melted when the light caught the tears glimmering in its large dark eyes.

"Hey, you look like you could use some help," she gently said.

She unzipped the small front pocket of her backpack and pulled out a set of tools that she used for working on the ship's circuit boards. Shining the light on the lock, she tried to balance it as she pulled free the tool she would need. She blinked in surprise when a pair of small hands reached out and took the light. Four tiny fingers held the light on the lock for her.

"Thank you!" she breathed.

Bending forward, she worked the tool into the lock, poking around until she felt the groove for the release. With a skillful twist, she popped the heavy lock open. She grinned triumphantly as she pulled the lock off and opened the cage.

The former prisoner scurried out and onto her lap. She sat back on her haunches in surprise. The creature lifted its head. Through the dirty fur she could see the red light on a neck collar. Her eyes darkened with fury. This poor creature had been captured by black market poachers.

"Hang on, and I'll get this off you. Stay really still," she instructed.

Leaning over the creature, she carefully twisted the collar around so that the release was facing her. This lock was going to be tricky. It had a small explosive device that would kill the poor thing. The creature bowed its head and buried its face in her lap while she carefully picked at the lock.

She paused and wiped her damp palm on her pant leg. Ander had shown her how to disarm locks like this. Heck, he had taught her how to disarm just about every type of lock invented. He'd told her that you never know when you'll need to get into something—or out of it.

"There you go," she said when the light turned green and the collar popped open. "I think I'll take this back to the ship and tear it apart. I might find out where it came from."

The creature looked up at her and tilted its head as if it understood and was thoughtfully considering her. She giggled in return. Its large, rounded ears twitched back and forth, and Raia affectionately scratched the soft fur on top of its head before gently lifting it and placing it on the ground.

Pulling her backpack toward her, she unzipped it and placed the collar inside. Ander might know which poachers used a device like this. He knew all kinds of cool things. She grinned when the other creature grabbed her hand and looked at it.

"No, you can't have my ring. Ander gave it to me," she said, curling her fingers when the furball tried to pull the white gold and diamond ring off.

She gasped softly when the furball laid its tiny hand on hers. Images floated through her mind—images that were coming from the creature. She frowned in confusion. Ander had never told her about any telepathic animals.

A beep startled her and the two creatures. She scowled down at the communicator on her wrist, rolling her eyes when she saw Ander's blue-green, scaly face scowling back at her. Pushing up off the ground, she glanced both ways along the alley before she answered.

"Hey, Ander," she cheerfully greeted.

The scowl on his face darkened. "Go down the alley away from the market, turn left, and I'll meet you," he ordered.

"Aw, Ander," she complained. "I haven't found a present yet!"

"Given the commotion the Tiliqua is causing, you've had enough excitement," he dryly replied.

She rolled her eyes again, forgetting that he could see her, and kicked at a piece of litter on the ground. "I didn't do anything," she muttered.

Ander's expression softened. "I know you didn't. Come meet me. I have something I think you might like."

"Okay," she mumbled, disconnecting the connection and sighing loudly.

Turning around, she frowned when she noticed that both of the cute but bizarre creatures had disappeared while she was talking to Ander. She huffed out a heavy sigh and shrugged her shoulders in disappointment. It was probably just as well. Ander had a strict rule of no animals on the ship.

She reached down, zipped her backpack up, and slung it over her right shoulder. Her foot hit the cage, and she looked down at it with a frown. Biting her lip in indecision, she cast a sweeping scan of the area. The last thing she wanted was for the spotted animal, or maybe the mischievous fur ball, to get trapped again.

Halfway down the alley was a recycling chute. Pleased with her idea, she picked up the small metal cage, pulled open the refuse box and deposited the offending cage down the chute. Wiping her hands, she took off down the alley, pausing when she reached the end to peer around the corner before turning left. A wry smile curved her lips when Ander straightened from where he had been leaning against the wall. She nodded toward the box and a colorfully wrapped package in his arms.

"Did you find what you were looking for?" she asked.

He smiled and nodded. "Yes, Happy Birthday, Raia," he said, holding out the wrapped package.

"What did you get me? Can I open it now?" she asked with a huge grin.

She eagerly skipped toward him and reached for the thick package. Shaking it gently to see if it rattled, she tested the weight, trying to guess what was inside. It felt solid. Ander chuckled, wrapped his tail around her waist, and pulled her into a tight hug.

"Happy Birthday," he muttered before releasing her.

She grinned up at him. "Thanks, Ander," she said.

"Do you want me to carry it?" he asked.

She shook her head. "No, I can carry it," she replied, hugging her gift against her chest.

He chuckled again and placed his arm around her shoulders. "So, are you going to tell me what happened?" he asked.

She sighed loudly. "I swear it was so weird!" she began, walking beside him as he turned around and they retraced their steps back to the docking bays.

CHAPTER TWO

𝒫i paused and waited for Chummy. The small, fluffy, brown and white Marica Peekaboo wiggled her nose at her hesitant companion. Chummy was favoring his front right paw. She didn't miss Chummy's worried glance at the young creature standing with the large Tearnat. Nor did she miss the way Chummy's fur stood up on the back of his neck when the large reptilian reached out, wrapped his tail around the young girl's waist, and pulled her against him. She placed a paw against Chummy's side to calm him.

He not hurting her. Look, she happy, Pi silently conveyed.

Raia... I like her, Chummy replied.

She good. We keep her, Pi said, turning her large, warm, dark chocolate-colored eyes to Chummy.

Chummy rubbed his head against her in agreement. Pi could sense the Quazin Chumloo's exhaustion, pain, and fear. In her daily search for food and treasures, she had discovered Chummy in the back storeroom of the Tiliqua's shop. Pi didn't need her ability to see the future to know what would have happened to Chummy. The Tiliqua was going to kill him and use his unusual fur to make a wrap for one of the wealthy patrons living on Sanapare.

Even though she had whisked Chummy away using her ability to teleport, she couldn't open the cage or remove the deadly collar around his neck. She had spent the morning scouring the area for the key or a tool she could use to unlock the cage. In her last search for the key in the Tiliqua's shop, she had spotted the young girl and known immediately that their destinies were entwined.

What about the Tearnat? Chummy uneasily inquired.

Pi studied the reptilian being and wiggled her nose. He wouldn't be happy once he found them, but she also knew he wouldn't harm them —or do anything to upset Raia. Still, her visions weren't always right.

We be safe, Pi reassured Chummy.

Chummy snorted and shook his head. *I not so sure*, he grumbled.

Pi snickered, turned, and pulled Chummy against her when he sagged. She knew which ship the girl and Tearnat were going to, and quickly visualized the docking tube. With the image firmly in her mind, their bodies shimmered, and then they vanished.

Chummy shook his head to clear the dizziness and slid off of Pi's back.

I no like it when you poppies in and out, he thought as he flopped over onto his back and stared up at the metal ceiling.

A noise to his left made him look, and he flashed a weak smile when Pi snorted at him and shook her head. Tilting his head to follow Pi's movements, he watched with amusement as she explored what was obviously Raia's bedroom.

She disappeared and reappeared with dizzying speed. It reminded him of the first time he'd seen her several days ago. He'd been barely aware of her at first because of the drugs the trappers had used.

He blinked when Pi appeared beside him and laid her hand against his brow. He could sense her concern for him and emitted a small, reassuring purr. The last of his fear drained away when she shared the vision of their future together with Raia.

You sure? he asked, staring up at her with hope-filled eyes.

I sure, she confidently replied.

The sound of footsteps and voices echoed along the corridor outside the cabin. He rolled onto his belly and sat up, warily watching the door. Pi crawled up next to him, listening as well. Raia and the Tearnat continued past the cabin without stopping.

What we do now? he asked.

Pi gazed at him with twinkling eyes. *You sleep. I explore,* she said with a mischievous grin.

Chummy wrinkled his nose when Pi suddenly disappeared again. He lifted his injured paw to his mouth and licked the wound he'd received from his attempts to escape the cage. Lowering his paw, he yawned and sleepily blinked as he carefully studied the room. A large, fluffy red pillow on the bed enticed his curiosity, making him wonder if it was as soft as it looked.

With a wiggle of his nose, the pillow rose off the bed and floated down to the floor, landing in front of him. He placed his front paws on the pillow and pushed it across the floor and under the bed. With one last nudge, he climbed onto the pillow, circled three times, and settled down with a purr of contentment.

We have a good pet, he thought with a happy sigh.

∽

Raia placed the last of the dishes in the sanitizer before she wiped down the counter and table. Tossing the damp towel next to the sink, she picked up the birthday gift Ander had given her from the bench seat and exited the galley. She walked along the narrow corridor to the bridge. Climbing the three steps, she plopped into the co-pilot seat, resting one leg over the arm of the chair, and stared out into deep space.

"I'm sorry we couldn't stay any longer," Ander gruffly said after a few minutes of silence.

She sighed and shrugged. "There wasn't much to see. Most of the junk there was way overpriced," she replied.

"I hope you like your gift," he said.

She looked down at the heavy book on her lap and traced a finger across the battered cover. The gift was typical of Ander. She opened the book, flicking through the pages.

"It's great, Ander. What girl wouldn't want a copy of—" She paused and studied the writing. It had been a while since she had read this language. "—*The Complete History of the United States and the Con— Constitution*," she mumbled with a frown. "Where is the United States?" she asked.

Ander paused, and she studied his face. "It's about the planet where I found you," he quietly answered.

She looked at him in surprise. "I thought you said you bought me from an Antrox because I was too boney to be used for Pactor food," she said.

"Yeah, well, I wanted to wait until you were old enough to understand what really happened," he responded.

She tilted her head and raised an eyebrow at him. "Don't you think the truth would have been better than letting me think I was about to be a Pactor snack?" she inquired.

He gave her a sharp-toothed grin and tapped the book on her lap with the tip of his tail. "I didn't want to scare you," he said.

She shook her head and sat back in her seat. "So, if I wasn't meant to be Pactor food, what is the truth?" she demanded.

Ander sighed, switched on the auto-pilot, and rose from his seat. With a wave of his hand, he motioned for her to follow him. She grunted and rose from her seat.

He exited the bridge and walked down the corridor to the far cabin, which he had converted into his office. The door opened, and she stepped in behind him. She stood at the door and watched as he walked over to a set of storage drawers.

The room was filled with artifacts from all over the star systems. She was so used to all the different pieces that she had never really thought about the significance of each relic. She had grown up digging in dirt on far-off planets and visiting less discriminating shops on hundreds of asteroid mines and Spaceports scattered throughout the known galaxies.

"What are you looking for?" she asked.

Ander pulled a small box out of the drawer and wiped his large blue-green palm over the top. There was no dust on it thanks to the advanced filtration system he had installed when he purchased the freighter.

She stepped closer when he set the box on the built-in desk and took off the lid. Curious, she put her book down next to the box and peered inside. On top was a small leather wallet.

She reached in and pulled it out. She turned it over in her hands, examining it before she opened it. Inside, there was a plastic card. She turned the wallet to study the image. Her breath caught as vague images filled her mind. Breathing through her mouth, she closed her eyes and tried to capture the memory.

"What do you remember?" he gently asked.

She hissed in frustration and shook her head. "The man is laughing. He is saying something funny. I—there's a bright light that hurt my eyes. I see a woman. She has long black hair, like me." She lifted her hand and touched her hair. "He was alone. I was crying because she wasn't there," her voice faded, and she looked at Ander with tears in her eyes.

Ander sighed, wrapped his arm around her shoulders, and pulled her against him. "He was your human father," he said.

She wiped away the tear sliding down her cheek. "What happened?" she demanded.

Ander released her and slowly pulled out the other items in the box. He placed each item in a row along the desk. The last one was a small, rag doll with black hair, button eyes, and a beautiful silk dress with a wide sash around her waist.

"I was caught off-guard near the Tirrella mining docks by some pirates. This was long after the Great War between the Sarafin, Curizan, and Valdier, but there was still a lot of cleaning up to do. The three Royal Houses were trying to stop the pirates who used the war as cover and were happy to continue fighting long after it was over. Anyway, all hell was breaking loose, and the Curizan warships chasing a small fleet of pirate ships weren't stopping for a research vessel which was in the wrong place at the wrong time. I made it to the jump gate, but my ship's navigation system had been damaged, and I was forced to do a manual override. A small miscalculation combined with a full charge of unstable Tirrella power crystals caused a surge as I passed through the gate. I ended up in an unknown star system, light years away from my planned trajectory. The damage, combined with the sudden burst of speed, sent me careening through that star system. I needed to find a planet where I could land and repair the damage. Fortunately, I crashed on the only planet in the region that was suitable for life, but—" he paused and took a deep breath.

"Your ship was the bright light," she guessed.

Ander nodded. "The opening I saw turned out to be a road. Your father was traveling down it. I barely pulled up in time to miss smashing into his vehicle, but he lost control and went over the side of a bridge. I landed a short distance away. I found the vehicle upside down in a shallow riverbed. Your father was killed instantly, but you were protected by the carrier you were strapped into. Once I saw your father and you, I knew I was in unknown territory," he explained.

She stared down at the image of her biological father. Her finger brushed against the tattered edge of the photo. She pulled it out. It was a photograph of the man, the woman she remembered, and herself as a baby. A wave of sadness filled her, but also curiosity about the woman.

"Why didn't you leave me?" she asked, looking up at him.

Ander's expression softened. "It was freezing cold out and my sensors showed no buildings or other forms of life suitable to leave you with for miles around. If I had left you, you would have died. I gathered what I could and took you back to my ship. I monitored the area for a few days as I worked on my ship, but no one came. If they had, I would have returned you to a place where you could have been found. Once I had the ship repaired, I decided to take you with me," he confessed in a gruff tone.

"Why?" she asked, touching his arm.

He looked down at her. She stepped into his embrace again when he wrapped his arms around her. She hugged him back.

"You got under my skin in a way nothing else ever had. You were my most treasured find, Raia. You always have been and you always will be," he said.

She laid her cheek against his chest. "I love you, Ander," she murmured.

"It isn't much, but these are all the things I salvaged from the vehicle," he said.

"Ander...?" she whispered.

"Yes, love?" he said.

"Thank you for not leaving me behind," she said in a voice filled with emotion.

"Never, girl. I would go to the farthest galaxies and back for you," he promised.

CHAPTER THREE

Raia shifted the heavy box in her arms and slowly walked to her cabin. Ander patted her on the shoulder as he continued back to the bridge. She adjusted the box, pressing it against the wall, and waved her hand across the display panel. She had demanded that Ander install one after he accidentally walked in on her changing clothes a few months ago.

She grinned at the memory. Ander's shocked expression, combined with his clumsy and startled retreat, still made her laugh. It was the first time she had ever seen the huge Tearnat literally tripping over his tail. The evening meal had been a little awkward.

She tightened her grip on the box and stepped into her cabin when the door slid open. This was the only spot on the ship that was all hers. Trinkets from all over the star systems filled her room. She had strung together her collection of tiny crystals along one wall. On another wall, she had mounted plaster casts embedded with the scales from the dragons found on Valdier. She had placed knickknacks from each of the spaceports on shelves on each side of her bathroom.

Dropping the box on her bed, she sat down on the edge. She moved aside the heavy book Ander had given her and opened the box. She paused, her hand in midair, when she noticed her big red fluffy pillow was missing.

Raia slowly lowered the lid to the bed and stood. This time, she took her time looking around her room. One of her jade figurines was missing from the top shelf. She walked over and touched the two remaining figurines. There used to be three Tasiers: a mommy, a daddy, and a baby. The baby was missing.

"Son of a—" she muttered.

There were six pieces missing from her various collections, but more than a dozen were moved. What didn't make any sense was that some of her more valuable pieces were left untouched. A scraping noise from behind sent a shaft of alarm through her. Whoever took her stuff was still in the room.

She felt around on the shelf next to her until she found the heavy iron sculpture of a Sarafin cat shifter in mid-transformation. Gripping it tightly, she held it out in front of her. She stared at the entrance to the bathroom.

"You'd better come out now!" she ordered.

She gaped in surprise when she heard the toilet flush followed by the sound of running water. She held the sculpture with both hands and slid along the wall toward the door leading out of her cabin. Whoever was here must have snuck on at the Spaceport.

She flinched when she heard a noise behind her. Near the door, she twisted around and hit a fragile crystal vase that Ander had given her last year for her birthday. It fell off the table, but before she could grab it, it floated out of her reach and landed back onto the table.

"What the Dragon's balls?" Raia cursed.

A movement out of the corner of her eye made her turn around again. She gawked in astonishment when the items in the box on her bed began to spill over the side as if they had a life of their own.

Completely intrigued instead of afraid now, she placed the iron sculpture on the desk and walked back over to her bed.

"You!" she breathed, staring down at the tan and white fur ball that had gotten her into trouble back on the spaceport.

She reached out and grabbed the rag doll as it rose out of the box. Her legs almost gave out under her when a small black and white fluff ball floated by. She stared at the small creature she had rescued as it floated upside down past her before plopping down on her pillow with a squeal of delight.

"Both of you— I... you can— Oh, boy! I'm going to be in so much trouble with Ander," she breathed out with a shake of her head before she burst out laughing.

The tan and white fur ball was now peering over the edge of the box. On its head it wore a pair of pink, animal-pattern underpants.

Raia reached down to pull the brightly colored bloomers off the creature's head. When she touched it, a swift tingling feeling engulfed her, and she glanced back and forth between the two creatures on her bed. Images flashed through her mind. She kept looking back and forth between the creatures, trying to understand which one was sending her the images. As the pictures became clearer, she began to understand the broken bits of language mixed in with them. It took her a minute to piece the words together.

"*Chimaigchi tie mol lot,*" 'You speak Chimaigchi!' she repeated in a shocked tone.

Chummy nodded. *We speak many languages,* he replied.

Pi continued going through the items in the box. She reached for the leather wallet and opened it. Raia watched with a bemused expression as the inquisitive creature began pulling items out of the slim pockets.

"Who— what are you... and you?" she asked, looking back and forth between the two animals.

Chummy rolled into a sitting position and tilted his head. *I Chummy. That Pi. She a Marica Peekaboo*, he responded with a grin.

"Chummy—and Pi. I don't think I've ever heard of a Marica Peekaboo before," she mused, looking at the black and white furry creature that was now fluffing her pillow. "What species are you?"

I a Quazin Chumloo, Chummy answered.

Raia looked back and forth between the two, then she leaned over and rescued the items Pi had pulled out of the wallet. She didn't have a clue what she was going to do with the two creatures. Ander was sure to have a fit when he saw them.

"What are you doing here?" she finally asked.

Pi poked her head up over the side of the box again and stared at her with wide, somber eyes. Raia watched as the Marica Peekaboo clambered over the side of the box, holding the picture of her biological parents and her as a young child in tiny fingers. Pi scooted over to her on three legs and climbed onto her lap.

Chummy walked across the bed and touched her arm with his paw. *You family now,* he said mentally.

Raia gulped when she saw flashes of herself and the two creatures. These images were different—They were together somewhere that she didn't recognize. It was like she was seeing herself in the future.

"I've got to tell Ander about you guys," she whispered.

Pi snorted and pulled the colorful bloomers back on her head with both of her ears sticking out of the leg openings. Chummy retrieved the rag doll and retreated to the pillow. She looked down at the picture Pi had pulled out of the wallet.

Family. It was just me and Ander. Now— she shook her head.

"This is *not* the birthday I was expecting," she muttered as she rose from the bed and started cleaning up the mess Pi had made. "I think

I'll wait until tomorrow to tell Ander about you guys. At least by then we'll be too far away to turn around."

The sound of low twin snores greeted her statement. Both creatures were sound asleep on her pillow. Chummy was sprawled out on his back with one paw tucked around the old rag doll while Pi was curled up against his side with one ear twitching through the opening of the bloomer. She shook her head and slid the box under her bed. Gathering her nightclothes, she retreated to the bathroom.

"Ander is going to love this," she muttered.

Ander checked the long-distance sensors for the hundredth time since leaving the Spaceport. So far, so good. They weren't being tracked at the moment, which meant if he was lucky, no one knew about the object he had secretly received.

He muttered under his breath as a twinge of guilt swept through him. His gift to Raia hadn't been completely honest. He knew if he gave Raia a book from her world—one that belonged to her biological father—that she would keep it. The artifact hidden in the spine of the book was another matter.

He doubted anyone would think to tear the book apart. The artifact hidden inside would be better lost than in the hands of the Marastin Dow Ruling Council that was probably searching for it.

He regretted not being able to explore the origins of the artifact in greater depth until a later time. The message on the tiny folded scrap of paper included with the crystal was ambiguous and clear to him at the same time.

Don't ask questions. Don't mention the item to anyone. Hide it at all costs. Millions of lives depend on it.

The message promised danger, and he would never purposely expose Raia to that if he could help it. He softly groaned and shook his head as he realized he had done exactly that by hiding the crystal in the book he had given her. First thing in the morning, he would retrieve the book, remove the crystal, and hide it someplace far away from her.

Berman, what in the name of the stars have you gotten me into this time? he wondered, staring out into space.

He and the Marastin Dow had crossed paths many times through their shared interest in history, but Ander had left behind the dangerous – and infinitely more lucrative – expeditions after Raia had come into his life, and that had meant leaving behind Berman.

He tiredly ran a hand down his face, then set the ship on auto-pilot and rose from his seat. Exiting the bridge, he strode back to the galley. He needed a cup of tea to help soothe the nagging feeling of impending doom knotting his stomach.

He sighed loudly as he brewed a cup of Mythroot. This was one of the few items a replicator could never do justice in recreating. Brewing it the old-fashioned way in the antiquated tea kettle he had purchased years ago always gave him a sense of pleasure and calm.

"Berman, what have you found? And how much trouble is it going to cause?" he murmured, trying to decipher the mystery.

He poured the tea into a tall mug. Turning to the right, he opened the tall, cold storage unit.

"*Trinorsis helo!*" he exclaimed, jumping back nearly a foot.

He stared in disbelief at a small tan and white creature holding his favorite milk. It looked back at him with large eyes. He gritted his teeth together when the creature's tongue made a slow pass along its upper lip, cleaning the thick and creamy liquid that had formed a small white mustache.

"Oh, no, you don't! How in the name of Tearraid did you get on my ship?" he demanded.

He reached out to grab the creature, but it disappeared before he could wrap his hand around its neck. Thankfully, he caught the jug of milk before it spilled. He righted the container, closed the door, and whirled around, scanning the kitchen. He gaped, his mouth open wide, when he saw another creature, this one with black and white markings covering its body.

"You miserable rodent. That's my tea!" he snapped.

The creature was lapping up the tea. He strode forward and grabbed his mug, holding it protectively between his palms. The sound of crunching made him scowl with annoyance. He jerked open the cabinet above the counter. The disappearing fur ball from the cold storage unit was now devouring the special cookies that Willia had given him. He reached in and tried to take the bag from the creature.

"Those are mine!" he growled, tugging on the bag.

He cursed again when the bag ripped. He watched in horror as his prized cookies were tossed into the air. The horror turned to aggravation when the hot tea in his hand splashed out, soaking his shirt and heating the scales on his chest. He stumbled back several feet, holding the mug of steaming liquid at arm's length.

Stunned disbelief flashed through him when the cookies danced in midair before floating upward. The black and white creature stepped off the counter and hovered in the air—plucking the cookies out of it and munching on them while the other creature resumed its foraging in the cabinet.

The moment of surprise gave him time to study the two creatures again. They looked vaguely familiar, like he had seen them before, but couldn't quite put his finger on what they were. The tan and white one disappeared and reappeared in several places. He pursed his lips when he saw it sitting at the dining table with the jug of milk between its hands.

He smiled in amusement as the names of the creatures finally hit him. "Marica Peekaboo—and you are a—Quazin Chumloo," he finally said.

The two creatures paused and studied him before resuming their destruction of his galley. Well—more like their attack on his favorite food and beverage. He shook his head. He had heard of both species—even seen a Marica Peekaboo once in the wild. The Marica Peekaboo were damn near impossible to capture. He realized why now. The damn things could teleport!

He turned his attention to the Quazin Chumloo. Those were exceedingly rare. He had only seen holograms of them. Their ability to blend in with their natural surroundings was part of the reason, but he suspected the massive destruction of their habitat nearly a century ago was the biggest issue. He had been a part of the team sent to petition the Curizan Royal family to protect the creatures—even though the team he was on wasn't sure if any still existed. Now there was one floating in his galley.

"Warning. Long range sensors have detected two vessels approaching at a rapid speed. Vessel identification—eighty-five percent accuracy Class V Marastin Dow Battle cruisers," the tinny voice of the computer warned.

"Raia!" he roared as he tossed his partially filled mug into the sink.

Turning on his heel, he sprinted out of the galley and back to the bridge. "Raia! Wake up, girl. We've got company," he bellowed.

"I'm coming," she breathlessly called from her cabin door behind him.

CHAPTER FOUR

While Raia hurriedly dressed, adrenaline flowed through her, causing her heart to race. After she was ready, she jogged down the corridor in the direction of the bridge, skidding to a brief stop when she glanced through the door of the galley and saw Pi and Chummy. She cursed and shook her head.

"For once, I hope you are the company he is yelling about," she muttered.

"Raia! We have two Marastin Dow warships approaching fast," Ander yelled.

It felt like her heart dropped to her stomach. She pulled her gaze away from her two new furry friends and took off running for the bridge. Throwing herself into the co-pilot seat, she scanned the display.

"Can we outrun them?" she breathlessly asked.

Ander shook his head. "Not at the speed they are approaching. Our best hope is to get to the jump gate thirty clicks from here. If we can pass through it before they catch us, I can deploy some energy decoys," he grimly answered.

She wiped her damp palms against her pant legs. "Are there any Curizan warships nearby? We aren't that far from Sanapare. Surely, they should have one close to keep all the wealthy patrons safe from attacks," she suggested.

"There might be. Send out a distress alert," Ander said.

She reached for the communication display and pulled it up. "This is the *Explorer's Adventure* requesting immediate support. We are being pursued by two Marastin Dow warships in Curizan airspace. Again, this is the *Explorer's Adventure* requesting help. We are being pursued by two Marastin Dow warships in Curizan controlled space," she said.

"*Explorer's Adventure,* this is the Curizan Battle Cruiser *Dark Nebula.* We have received your request and are locking onto your position," came the immediate response.

Raia almost melted back in her seat with relief. "We are approaching Jump Gate 58735. We are...." She looked at Ander.

"Twenty-five clicks," he said.

"We are twenty-five clicks from the gate," she repeated.

"Maintain your progress. Please be advised that we are one hundred clicks from your position," the *Dark Nebula* communication tech replied.

"Please hurry," she whispered, watching the images of the two Marastin Dow ships on the tracking screen growing larger.

"They won't make it in time," Ander grimly stated.

Raia looked at him. "If we can get to the jump gate then we should be alright, won't we?" she asked.

"It will be close. At the rate the Marastin Dow ships are approaching—Raia, gather your emergency pack and get to the escape shuttle," he suddenly ordered.

She shook her head. "Ander—I'm not going to leave you," she retorted in a tight voice.

Ander shot her an emotion-filled glance before he returned his attention to the screen. "If we make it to the jump gate, you won't, but if we don't and the Marastin Dow board us… Raia, they don't take prisoners. I know their ways. I might be able to survive, but neither of us will live if they capture you. They will try to use you to control me—or worse, and I'll fight them to the death. I won't launch the shuttle unless there is no other choice," he vowed.

"You promise?" she said, leaning over to grip his arm.

"Have I ever lied to you?" he replied.

Her gaze softened. "Yes, but only when it was to protect me," she murmured.

"Go—and take the book I gave you and those two creatures in the galley with you," he instructed.

She nodded and rose to her feet. She paused at the doorway and looked at the display again. They were now ten clicks from the jump gate. Even without doing the math, she could tell the Marastin Dow ships would overtake them before they reached it.

"We are definitely going to add a weapons system to the EA if we make it," she said.

Ander released a strained chuckle. "If we live through this, I'm sure I'll never hear the end of your 'You should have listened to me' speech. Now go—and don't forget the book and those two rodents. And, that's going to be another thing we have to talk about," he called over his shoulder.

Raia nodded and jumped down into the corridor. She paused long enough at the galley door to look for Pi and Chummy. They weren't there. She fervently hoped they were back in her cabin. There wouldn't be enough time to search the freighter for them if they weren't.

Placing her palm against the locking panel to her cabin, she slid past the door as it opened. She skidded to a surprised stop when she saw Pi and Chummy on her bed with her emergency bag. Pi was shoving the book Ander had given her a few hours ago into the top of the bag. Chummy was sitting beside it with his tiny legs wrapped around the rag doll.

She stumbled forward when the freighter violently shuddered. Alarms blared and the automatic fire-retardant system activated. A second explosion sent her sprawling toward the bed. She would have done a face-plant if she hadn't thrust her arms out at the last second.

"Go to the shuttle," she hissed.

Pi wrapped her arms around Chummy and the two disappeared. Raia twisted on the bed and pushed herself up. She closed the bag with trembling fingers, straightened, and slung it over her shoulder. A wild glance around her cabin made her regret not having another bag. She reached out and grabbed a box of Tirrella power crystals and stuffed it into the side pocket of her backpack.

"Raia, get to the shuttle now!" Ander ordered over the communicator.

"I'm almost there," she lied.

She darted through the open door and down the corridor. At the end, she pulled open a hatch. Twisting around, she climbed down through the opening, pausing just long enough on the fourth step to close and seal the hatch behind her. She grasped the support handles and slid the rest of the way down the ladder.

Her boots clanged loudly against the metal floor as she landed. She released her grip on the supports and took off running back toward the front of the ship. The shuttle was tucked midway between the freighter's bow and stern.

Another explosion sent her careening into the wall. She grunted, reached out, and steadied herself. Small fires flared up and were quickly extinguished by the fire-retardant system. Unfortunately, the venting system must have been damaged because smoke was filling the corridor.

Coughing, Raia covered her mouth and nose with her jacket sleeve. Tears from the acrid smoke filled her eyes, partially blinding her. She stumbled along the corridor until she reached the shuttle hatch. Laying her palm against the panel, she impatiently waited for the security system to acknowledge her.

She half-fell through the door when it opened. Chummy and Pi were already there waiting for her. Turning, she slapped her palm to close the door behind her. A series of choking coughs gripped her. She slid the backpack off her shoulder with trembling fingers as she struggled to take a deep breath.

"And-Ander, I'm in-in the shuttle," she wheezed.

"They've taken out the main engine. There is no way to outrun them now. Find a village called Galax on the Ceran-Pax home world. You'll be safe there," Ander instructed.

"Ander—" she said, trying to hide the fear in her voice.

"You can do this, Raia. Remember everything I've taught you. Don't trust anyone—and I mean *anyone*! Even those you think I was friends with. Keep those two rodents with you. They can help you now. I love you, girl. If I survive, I'll come for you. I promise," he said.

Raia tried to speak, but her voice failed her. She didn't know if it was the smoke or emotion. She reached out and steadied herself when she heard the shuttle bay doors open. Forcing herself to move, she hurried to the shuttle bridge and slid into the pilot seat.

As if on automatic-pilot, she ran through the checklist, fired up the small but powerful engines, pulled the safety harness over her shoulders, and secured it. Her fingers trembled as she entered the coordinates that Ander was giving her. A shudder ran through her when she felt the shuttle clamps retract, and the shuttle dropped.

"I love you, Ander," she choked out.

Seconds later, she was shooting under the freighter. Her breath caught when she saw how close the two Marastin Dow warships were to them. The shuttle was indistinguishable among the floating debris from the freighter cast out by the Marastin Dow blasts and the refuse that Ander had discharged to help camouflage her escape.

When she was three clicks away from the jump gate, she powered up the engines to full and pushed the shuttle as fast as it would go. The lights flashed as she entered the jump field. She was thrust back against the seat, and the world turned into a kaleidoscope of colorful streaks. A shuddering sob escaped her and tears streaked down her cheeks as her world crumbled around her.

CHAPTER FIVE

*S*ix months later:
   Village of Galax, Ceran-Pax

"Any sign of her?" Raia asked, peering through the digital ocular lens.

Chummy nodded. *She coming back,* he replied.

Raia kept her focus on the strange couple walking through the village. For the last six months, she, Pi, and Chummy had kept their distance from all the local inhabitants. Ander's words about not trusting anyone still rang clearly in her mind.

She narrowed her eyes when the man who looked a lot like her in many ways bent over and picked up a little girl and placed her on his shoulders. The couple and the child were laughing.

Pi say they no hurt us, Chummy said.

Raia pursed her lips, ignoring Chummy's comment. Pi and Chummy had been insisting for months that the two men who looked suspiciously like her could help them. She almost gave in—until she saw the two purple women.

"They are with the Marastin Dow. Have you forgotten what the Marastin Dow did to Ander?" she growled.

She scooted back as Pi suddenly appeared next to them. Rolling into a sitting position, she took the bag that Pi had taken with her and began going through the items. She lifted her eyebrow at Pi and pulled out a loaf of fresh bread and a large orange fruit.

"I showed you the tools I needed. We don't need food. We have plenty of that. I need a splicer. The one I showed you is burnt out," she said with a roll of her eyes as she stuffed all the items back into the bag.

Pi wiggled her nose and reached out for the piece of fruit with a pleading expression. Raia tried not to smile, but it was impossible. Over the last six months, she had discovered Pi had an insatiable appetite—especially for fruit, and milk. She also loved shiny objects. Chummy, on the other hand, loved Mythroot tea and cookies.

The smile on her lips faded as she thought of Ander's favorite tea. Almost immediately, she felt Pi and Chummy's gentle touch. She closed her eyes and absorbed their support. She swallowed, pushing away the pain, and opened her eyes.

"I'll go later tonight and see if I can find a splicer. I shouldn't have asked you to look for one," she said.

Chummy looked worried. She reached out and gently scratched him behind his left ear. His back foot thumped against the ground with pleasure.

"I'll be alright. Pi isn't the only one who is good at disappearing," she teased.

She climbed to her feet and retrieved the bag. "Come on. It will be dark soon. If we're going to have a nice dinner with some fresh food instead of the replicated kind, we better get going. You two are lucky that

Ander taught me how to cook without a replicator or you would be out of luck," she said.

Pi clapped her front feet together with glee, while Chummy purred in agreement. Together, they returned to the small wooded area where the shuttle was located. Raia knew they wouldn't be able to stay there indefinitely without being found. She also knew that if Ander had survived the Marastin Dow attacks, he would have already made it to the village.

She needed to make some minor repairs to the shuttle and she needed to make some serious decisions. Galax looked like a nice village to visit, but there was no way she could stay there. She lifted her hand and gently fingered the intricately carved, rectangular crystal disk hanging from the black tungsten rope chain. She discovered the disk in the spine of the book that Ander had given her for her birthday. The words inscribed on it reminded her of Ander.

Freedom without Bonds. Life without Fear.

The more she thought of the inscription, the more it resonated with her. She would live her life without fear and be free to do the things she wanted. The galaxy was a huge place. She was lucky enough to know where most of the out-of-the-way spots were—and how to negotiate with the different traders and merchants, thanks to Ander.

"Once I repair the shuttle and earn enough credits, I can sell it and buy a bigger ship. We'll start our own freighter business. I know the routes and most of Ander's connections. We'll explore the stars just like Ander did when he was younger," she said, talking more to herself than to her two friends.

She lifted her hand and scratched Chummy when he landed on her shoulder. The smile on her face grew the more she thought about her plans. Ander used to tell her stories of his explorations before he found her. She often dreamed of the adventures she would go on. There was no reason why she couldn't do it now. All it took was time, credits, a bigger ship—and a lot of luck.

∼

Later that evening, Raia crouched along the edge of the tall stalks of grain. She scanned the area, waiting for Pi to return from her scouting trip. Chummy clung to the backpack on her back.

Pi appeared next to her. *Man go inside house,* she said.

"Good. You two keep an eye out while I see if I can find the tools and parts I need in the work shed," she whispered.

She crept forward before darting to the large rounded shed. Pressing her back against the wall, she peered at the house. Through the open windows she could hear a child's giggle and two men talking. She drew back and pressed her hand against the panel.

"Who locks a shed in the middle of nowhere?" she groaned when the door didn't open.

She motioned for Pi. "Can you open it from inside?" she whispered.

Pi grinned, nodded, and disappeared. Seconds later, the door slid open. Chummy floated off of her shoulder to a nearby shelf.

"Since you two are with me, you might as well look for the splicer I showed you earlier," she instructed.

She shrugged her backpack off and held it in her left hand. The three of them silently moved around the room, examining the tools and parts on the benches and hanging on the wall. Raia picked up a bundle of wire, a gimbal block, a main Lox valve, and a heat exchanger and placed them in her backpack. She stared with envy at a larger heat exchanger and turbo-pump. Her pack wasn't big enough to carry them. A series of circuit boards on the workbench drew her attention, and she fingered them with a thoughtful expression. These went to a land skimmer, but with some minor tweaks, she could modify them for the shuttle's onboard system.

A crash behind her caused her to swivel around with a muttered hiss. Pi had knocked a bucket off the shelf, and it had landed on Chummy.

Now, her two mischievous cohorts were playing, with Pi sending the bucket around the room while Chummy steered it.

"Quiet! Do you want the farmers to hear us?" she hissed in annoyance.

"It is too late for that," a woman's voice dryly stated.

Raia turned again and faced the woman standing by a second door that she had missed seeing. She groaned when she saw the woman wasn't alone. The man she had seen earlier was standing beside her.

"Yeah… well… we'll just be going," she said, trying to step toward the open door.

"I think not. What are you doing here?" a second man stated.

"Nothing," Raia answered, defiantly lifting her chin at the man's gruff tone.

She clutched her backpack to her chest. Chummy hurried over to her, climbed up her legs, and clung to her neck while Pi vanished. It didn't help that the Quazin Chumloo had found the splicer she was searching for and was trying to stuff it into her bulging backpack.

"That's an old splicer and doesn't work very well. There's a better one on the third shelf," the man said, walking past her to retrieve the newer splicer.

"Ben, I just bought that one!" the other man complained.

Raia warily backed up when the man named Ben turned and held out the splicer. Chummy paused and looked at the shiny new splicer and then down at the old one that looked like it had seen better days. She groaned when the little Quazin Chumloo held out the old splicer and eagerly accepted the new one.

The man named Ben paled and took a wary step back. "You're welcome," he said.

"What's wrong?" the woman demanded.

Ben shook his head. "Nothing, love. We were about to eat dinner. Would you like to join us?" he politely asked.

Raia shook her head. Pi reappeared in front of her, standing on the backpack next to Chummy, gripped her cheeks between his palms, and forced her head up and down in agreement. The two men and woman chuckled at Pi's passionate response. Raia released a small groan.

"Pi loves to eat," she mumbled through her squished lips.

"Hanine's going to love the way he can disappear and reappear. It reminds me of...," the other man's voice faded.

"She—Pi is a girl. Chummy is a boy," Raia said, pulling her face free. "I... guess we could eat something."

"Hanine, you can put the weapon away," the woman called out.

"I already did," Hanine responded, stepping out of the shadows.

Raia swallowed as she stared into the face of the other Marastin Dow. She started to back up but stopped when the man took a step forward. Chummy laid his tiny paw against her cheek.

They no hurt us.

The Quazin Chumloo's silent message flowed through her mind. She wasn't sure if she should trust the Quazin Chumloo's judgement or not. The memories of what the Marastin Dow had done to their freighter were still too fresh.

"I'm Ben Cooper. That's my brother, Aaron, my wife, Evetta, and Aaron's wife, Hanine," Ben introduced.

Raia followed his gestures as he introduced each person. She couldn't help but be curious about the two men who looked a lot like her—yet different—and their relationship with the two Marastin Dow women. She blinked when a small head popped up over Hanine's shoulder.

"Baba," the little girl said, reaching out a hand.

Raia could see the little girl was staring with wide, bright, curious eyes at Chummy and Pi. Before she could stop him, Chummy floated up off the backpack. Raia reached out and grabbed the splicer before he dropped it. The chorus of soft surprised breaths mixed with the little girl's squeal of delight when Chummy floated over to her.

"Seriously! You brought Nayua with you?" Aaron demanded, striding over to Hanine.

Hanine raised an eyebrow at him. "Well, I couldn't very well leave her alone in the house. You know she is at the age where she gets into everything," she retorted.

Aaron took the laser rifle from Hanine and threaded his fingers through hers. Raia watched with a bemused expression as the couple exited the workshop quietly arguing over the fact that maybe Hanine could have remained in the house where it was safe.

"Not all Marastin Dow are the same," Ben quietly said.

Raia nodded and pushed the splicer down into her backpack. Pi had disappeared again. She was probably exploring the inside of the house by now.

"I can barter for the splicer. I have some jade and Tirrella crystals," she blurted out.

Ben slid his arm around Evetta's waist and shook his head. "Don't worry about it. You know, if you need some help with the repairs to your ship, all you have to do is ask. All four of us are pretty good at repairs," he offered.

"Hanine is a genius if you need any programming work," Evetta added.

"If I need help, I'll ask," Raia replied.

They walked in silence to the house. She paused on the stairs and looked around. The house was huge with a wide front porch and chairs that rocked. The house reminded her of some of the ones in the book Ander had given her.

"What species are you?" she blurted out.

Ben paused on the top step and looked down at her. "Human... just like you," he answered.

"But... I look different from you," she said, climbing a step.

She looked up at him. He dropped his arm from Evetta's waist and a brief, silent communication passed between the two of them. Evetta smiled at her before disappearing into the house. He motioned to a set of chairs.

Raia remained where she was until he sat down in one of the chairs and began to rock. She slowly climbed the steps and walked over to the chair next to him. Placing her backpack on the porch, she sat down on the edge of the rocker and waited.

"I suspect you have Pacific Islander or Asian heritage. Aaron and I are —were—from Kansas. How old were you when you were taken?" he asked.

"Ander thinks I was about four. He said it is hard to tell because people age differently depending on their species. He had never seen a human before," she explained.

"Who is Ander?" Ben asked.

Tears burned her eyes, and she looked away, staring out over the large fields. "He was my father," she replied in a tight voice.

"Was? How long have you been alone?" he inquired.

Raia could hear the compassion in his voice. She wrapped her fingers around the strap of her backpack and tried to decide how much she should tell him. Chummy said that they could trust him. Pi would have warned her if they were in danger. She swallowed and cleared her throat.

"Six months... give or take a few weeks," she admitted.

"What's your name?" Ben asked.

She blinked in surprise, forgetting that she had never told them. "Raia... You can just call me Raia," she said, reluctant to tell him anything else.

"You are welcome to stay here. We've got plenty of room," he offered.

"Ben, dinner is ready," Evetta called from inside.

"We'll be right there," he replied.

"Well, you'd better hurry or there won't be anything left. The two beasts are almost done with their first plate of food," she warned.

Ben chuckled. "We'd better go inside," he said, rising to his feet.

Raia stood as well, unsure of what was going on. "Why are you being so nice?" she demanded.

Ben slowly turned and looked at her. There was a slight smile on his lips, but his eyes held a mixture of sadness and a hard edge. She tightened her grip on the backpack as she waited once again for his reply.

"We've been where you are now. If we can help make it easier on you, then so be it," he answered.

He pulled open the door and waited for her to go ahead of him. She slowly walked forward, pausing as she passed him. She scanned the interior of the home. The sound of Nayua giggling, and trying to talk, intermingled with the voices of Evetta, Aaron, and Hanine.

"Thank you," she murmured, glancing at him before she entered the house.

CHAPTER SIX

"Are you sure this is what you want to do, Raia? You are welcome to stay with us. Nayua has fallen in love with you and your creatures," Hanine said.

"They love her, too. It's just—I'm not used to being in one place for so long," Raia confessed, looking up from where she was working on the wiring of the new defense system Hanine was installing for her.

She smiled reassuringly at the purple-skinned woman who she had grown to like over the past four months. Her wariness of the two sisters slowly dissolved as the days turned into weeks and the weeks into months. Ben and Aaron had helped her make the repairs, then trade up the shuttle for a used freighter.

Hanine and Evetta took over after the purchase. Raia grinned at the memory of the two women chewing out their spouses for buying a piece of Tiliqua shit. They had insisted on taking over the renovation project after that and tackled the freighter with a thoroughness, expertise, and attention to detail that would have made Ander proud.

Fortunately for her, Pi had discovered a small fortune aboard the shuttle before she traded it in. Ander must have stockpiled the items in case they ever needed to use the shuttle as an escape—or he may have thought that the pirates would never think to search the small shuttle for anything of value. Either way, the stash of credits and variety of precious crystals were enough to purchase the small freighter—and complete the much-needed upgrades and repairs. The only thing it didn't do was give her much of a cushion once she was in space. She would have to find some jobs for that.

"You need to be very careful. Trust no one… well, except for us," Evetta cautioned.

Raia felt like rolling her eyes. "I know. You, Hanine, and Ben have already said that—multiple times. The only one who hasn't said it is Aaron," she dryly retorted.

"You are very young. There are so many others who would take advantage of you," Evetta continued.

Raia put the splicer down and smiled at both women.

"I promise I'll be alright. Ander taught me well. Besides, I have Chummy and Pi," she teased.

Hanine shook her head. "Those two will eat you out of a year's worth of credits before you know what happened," she grumbled.

"You're just upset because you know Nayua is going to be heartbroken that you took away her partners in crime," Raia retorted with a grin.

"Don't remind me. I caught them raiding the pantry last night," Hanine groaned.

Evetta laughed out loud and Raia giggled. She had learned a lot about Chummy and Pi over the last ten months—including their more extraordinary skills. Pi had shared glimpses of the future. She could only see a day or two in advance, but she was never wrong.

Chummy, on the other hand, could tell a lot about a person from touching them. He shared tiny bits of information—including a lot about the two women helping her now.

"Have you two ever thought of going to the planet where Ben and Aaron came from?" she casually inquired.

Evetta looked at her with a surprised expression and shook her head. "No. It would be too dangerous," she replied.

"Why?" she asked.

Hanine pointed to her chest. "We look different. Aaron said the people of his world do not know that aliens truly exist. If we were to go there, it would frighten them, and they would do horrible things to us. I would never put Nayua in that type of danger. It's bad enough being a Marastin Dow, but at least we can live here in peace," she said.

"Why are the Marastin Dow so mean?" she blurted out. "I know you aren't, but why are they—"

She lowered her head and looked at the tool she was holding. Talking about Earth and the Marastin Dow reminded her of Ander. Her chest hurt thinking about the fact that she would never see him again. She blinked the moisture from her eyes and looked up at Evetta when the woman placed a hand on her arm.

"Not all Marastin Dow are mean. There is a growing number who want change. In fact, most of our people want to live in peace. Our world is controlled by a small number of council members and military commanders who rule through fear, intimidation, and hatred. They know that as long as they keep us divided, they can control us. When we escaped...." Evetta looked at her sister then back at Raia. "When we escaped, there was talk of a revolution. The Science Officer on our ship was gathering a group to join the Resistance. He was betrayed, and we were all going to be sentenced to death. Hanine and I knew that Ben and Aaron would be killed immediately. The rest of us would have been made an example of. Many of our people have been murdered since. The only reason we have remained safe is because of the Curizan Prince Ha'ven Ha'darra. This village is a sanctuary for any who wish to live here. He has kept us protected," Evetta explained.

"Aaron said that the Marastin Dow are not unlike the humans known as Spartans," Hanine added.

Raia frowned. "Humans are like the Marastin Dow?" she asked in surprise.

Both women nodded. "At one time. Ben said the place he came from had a document that guided them. I do not remember what it was called. I know that Behr... that the Science Officer asked many questions about it. Unfortunately, Ben and Aaron remember little about the document," Evetta said with a sigh.

"They were very young when they left their planet and Aaron said neither were very interested in the school they attended," Hanine added.

Raia nodded, lost in thought. Humans were like the Marastin Dow. She looked down at her hand, turning it and studying her skin. It was darker than Ben and Aaron's tan complexions. Her eyes were slightly different—more almond-shaped, her nose a little wider, and her lips fuller. Her hair was a thick wave of midnight black where their hair was dark brown with a hint of red in the sunshine.

"Hey, Hanine! Ben and I finished the final adjustment on the bay door. Do you want to test it to make sure it seals all the way? We'd hate for Raia's britches to fall open when she takes off," Aaron hollered from the end of the corridor.

Hanine shook her head. "I swear I have no idea what he is saying half the time. He better not have left Nayua alone with those two creatures of yours," she muttered.

Raia laughed. She returned her focus to the defense system. There was still a lot of work to be done, but they were slowly getting there. She would miss the women. It was the first time in her life that she had spent so much time with someone of the same sex.

But I miss the freedom of the stars more, she thought as she finished soldering the connection on the circuit board.

The memory of Ander's gentle voice swept through her. *The universe is too large to stay in one spot. Hit the button, Raia. We've got places to explore.*

Yes, I do, Ander, she silently thought with a small, sad smile.

Two months later:

"Pi! Where are you? Chummy! You better come out here right now!" Raia growled.

"I hear giggles," Ben called out.

"Thank goodness!" Hanine murmured, lifting a hand to her chest.

Raia followed the sound to the refurbished galley. "Nayua, where are you?" she called in a sing-song voice, knowing the little girl would answer her.

"Rai-Rai, find me," Nayua sang back.

Raia smiled and walked over to the tall storage cabinet. She slowly pulled it open. Inside on the bottom shelf was a pile of blankets, toys, snacks, Nayua with Chummy in her arms, and Pi. She knelt down and grinned.

"Found you," she said.

"Go bye-bye," Nayua said, squeezing poor Chummy in her chubby arms.

"No, you no go bye-bye," Hanine retorted, reaching around Raia for her daughter.

Raia stood and stepped back as Nayua's face crumpled. She carefully extracted Chummy from the crying girl's arms. Chummy reached out and touched Nayua. The high-pitched screech froze and the little girl's face brightened when Pi reappeared holding Raia's rag doll. Nayua loudly sniffed and reached for the doll.

Raia opened her mouth to protest before closing it. The little girl was gently cradling the rag doll in her arms and rubbing her cheek against the soft strands of yarn. She reached out and ran her hand along Nayua's damp cheek.

"Nayua—" Aaron began.

Raia shook her head. "No, she can have it. It will be nice to know it is in a safe place—and well loved," she said.

"Are you sure?" Hanine asked with a concerned expression.

Raia looked at Hanine and smiled. "Yes, I'm sure," she said.

"My Rai-Rai," Nayua mumbled, sliding her thumb between her lips and laying her head on Hanine's shoulder.

"We'd better get her to bed," Aaron gently suggested, lifting his tired daughter into his arms. He looked at her. "Safe travels, Raia. If you are ever in the area or if you ever need anything, you know where to find us."

"Thanks, Aaron," she said.

Hanine wavered for a moment before she stepped forward and gave her a stalwart hug. "Don't trust anyone and keep the transporter device I gave you with you at all times," she murmured near Raia's ear.

"I will," Raia promised.

Hanine nodded before she turned and exited the galley with Aaron and Nayua. Raia pushed her trembling hands into her jacket pockets so that Evetta and Ben couldn't see them. She breathed deeply and forced a smile on her lips.

"I'll be alright," she insisted, gazing back at the twin pairs of worried eyes.

"Review the weapons system. It is automated, and I've programmed it to your voice commands," Evetta said.

"I have the vidcoms you and Hanine created for me. I'll go over them every night until I can operate it in my sleep," she promised.

"This isn't much, but we pooled together some credits that should keep you going for a bit. Be careful at the Spaceports. Dock at the higher levels. They have more security," Ben instructed.

Raia laughed. "I've probably been to more Spaceports than you and Aaron, Ben. I'll be okay," she promised.

Ben stepped forward and wrapped his arms around her. She pulled her hands free of her pockets and returned his embrace. Evetta wrapped her arms around the two of them.

"Keep those two creatures with you. Safe travels, Raia," Evetta murmured, before she released Raia and Ben and hurriedly followed her sister and Aaron.

Ben slid his arms down and cupped her hands. He squeezed them when he felt them tremble. Tears burned her eyes. Over the last four months, she had felt an especially close bond with Ben. He reminded her a lot of Ander with his quiet words and knowing looks.

"Don't be a stranger, Raia," he said.

She swallowed and nodded. "Thank you for all your help," she replied softly.

"If you ever need us, we'll be there for you," he promised.

"I know," she said in a voice thick with emotion.

"Besides, you'll need to come back to see your newest partner-in-crime," he teased, releasing her hands and shoving his hands in his pockets.

She frowned and looked at him with a confused expression. "What do you mean?" she asked.

The smile on his face grew. "Evetta and I are expecting a little one to give Nayua some company," he shared.

Joy filled her. She had been worried about Evetta the last few weeks. She knew the woman wasn't feeling well and was unusually tired. Now she knew why.

"That's awesome! I promise to keep in touch," she said.

Ben nodded, stepped forward, and kissed her on the forehead. "Just be careful out there and don't get into any trouble," he said in a stern tone before he turned on his heel and exited the room.

Raia stood still, listening as the bay hatch closed and sealed. The ship suddenly seemed extremely big and empty. Flexing her fingers, she breathed deeply until she felt the wave of panic recede.

"Pi, please tell me that I'm doing the right thing," she begged, kneeling until she was almost eye-level with the tan and white creature cuddling with Chummy.

Pi laid her tiny fingers on the back of Raia's hand. Images flashed through her mind and a sense of peace filled her. She looked at Chummy when he pressed his paw next to Pi's.

We go explore now? Chummy asked.

She smiled and nodded. "We go explore now. You two clean up this mess. I've got a ship to fly," she said, rising to her feet.

Striding out of the galley and down the corridor, she slid into the captain's chair on the bridge. This freighter might be old, but it was now in good shape. Running through the pre-flight checklist, she gripped the yoke, powered up the engines, and slowly lifted off the ground.

"Freedom without Bonds. Life without Fear," she vowed as she soared upward, disappearing through the atmosphere to whatever life had in store for her, Chummy, and Pi.

To Be Continued....

Behr's Rebel: Join Raia fourteen years later as she accepts a dangerous mission to rescue an imprisoned rebel leader that entangles her and her two powerful pets in a fight against the might of the Marastin Dow military.

BEHR'S REBEL

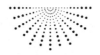

BEHR'S SYNOPSIS

Two battles: One fights for a cause; the other fights for survival...

General Behr De'Mar, leader of the Marastin Dow rebel forces, knows that it is only a matter of time before he is caught and executed. It doesn't matter to him. The cause he is fighting for is much larger than any one person—or so he thought.

Raia Glossman doesn't know what to think when she is hired by the strange, purple-skinned aliens. After all, the Marastin Dow are known for their cutthroat, kill anything-that-moves mentality. Why would they need a lone human woman to rescue their General? But credits are credits, and Raia never turns down a chance to earn a tidy sum. Besides, it seems like an easy job for her and her two innovative pets, Chummy and Pi. They'll get in, rescue the guy, collect their credits, and disappear again. The three of them perfected that little trick years ago. This time however, she is on the run with an army of Marastin Dow warriors on her tail! Not to mention that she is stuck with a tantalizing General, and she discovers she is the new poster-girl for the Marastin Dow Revolution. So much for anonymity!

Behr knows the moment he meets Raia and her two pets that they are special. Can he keep them alive and safe against the massive army threatening to end their hope of a new way of life, or will the history of the Marastin Dow's savagery doom them all?

CHAPTER ONE

Yardell Spaceport:
Present Day

"What'll you have?" the bartender called as she walked by.

"Ceran Slammer, no ice, with a twist of Yuckta juice," Raia answered as she threaded her way through the dimly lit bar to an empty corner table.

She picked the side of the table that would ensure her back was to the wall, and slid her backpack off her shoulder, placing it on the bench seat between the wall and the table. As she relaxed in the seat, her left hand rested on her blaster. The majority of her credits were safely tucked away in a small bag between her breasts.

She took a deep, calming breath and watched the bartender expertly prepare her drink. Less than a minute later, a robot server delivered her beverage. She pulled a couple of credits out of her jacket pocket and tossed them into the robot's small payment compartment. Leaning back in her seat again, she wrapped her fingers around her steaming drink and thoughtfully studied the other patrons under her lashes.

A heated argument at one of the gaming tables quickly turned violent. Using the distraction to her advantage, Raia reached down and opened the backpack's top compartment. Through the gap, she noted that Chummy had made himself a comfy little nest. The Chumloo was gnawing on a piece of fruit she had given him before they left the ship.

Pi wasn't back yet. Raia rolled her shoulders to ease the tension and lifted the glass of liquor to her mouth. She scanned the room, searching for Pi.

"Have you picked up anything interesting yet?" she casually inquired, hiding her moving lips behind the glass.

No, but man at bar thinking bad things. Woman sitting next to him looking for her mate. Tiliqua worry about business, Chummy replied.

Raia lifted an eyebrow. "What kind of bad thoughts is the man thinking?" she asked, warily studying the large male with a row of ridges down his back.

He think you pretty and wonder if he has enough credits, Chummy answered.

Raia curled her lip with disgust. She was *not* into guys with two tails. Shaking her head, she continued studying the patrons. Pi had foreseen Raia meeting her next commission here. Looking around at the crowd, she was beginning to wonder if her small friend might be losing her touch.

Man at bar coming, Chummy warned.

Raia silently groaned. She hated dealing with jerks—especially those of the big, mean-looking variety. She tilted her head back and warily observed the man as he approached her table.

There always seems to be one in the crowd, she grimly thought.

"Tibash je ta bay emo," 'Hey, pretty lady', the Bisnope greeted with a wide fat-lipped grin.

Raia laid her blaster on the table with the barrel aimed at the man's groin. She gave him a smile that didn't reach her eyes and shook her head.

"Maynish, ta ma bay," 'Keep moving, I'm not interested,' she replied.

The smile on his lips faded, and his eyes narrowed. She raised an eyebrow and shook her head in warning. With a flick of her thumb, she increased the power from a slight burn to a heated roast. The man's gaze flickered resentfully to the blaster.

"Rutahian ki shue lei," he jeered before turning and striding away.

He not nice, Chummy growled.

Just as Chummy said that, a light fixture above the man's head broke loose, swung down, and struck the man between the eyes. The man's head snapped back for a second before he fell backwards, knocked unconscious. The crowd paused, then resumed chatting as if nothing had happened. Two of the bar robots rushed over, lifted the man, and carried him out of the building.

And... that's what he gets for calling me a Rutahian whore, she mused.

She lowered her head, hiding the grin on her face. Hopefully, she was the only one who had seen Pi up near the light seconds before it fell. She adjusted her jacket, lifting one side to hide Pi's return.

"Thanks for that, but it really wasn't necessary. I had it under control," she stated in a dry tone.

Pi sniffed and climbed into her backpack next to Chummy. She placed the blaster on the seat next to her, and affectionately scratched Pi behind her ear. She was about to tell them that she was packing it in when a vision flashed through her mind.

They here, Chummy announced with a satisfied snort.

Raia's eyes narrowed as she studied the three cloaked figures at the entrance to the bar. The three new arrivals scanned the room before their focus narrowed on her. With a deep sigh, she lifted a hand and motioned to the server. The robot whizzed through the crowd before jerking to a halt in front of her.

"I'd like a large fruit platter with a side of Muza cream," she ordered.

"Twenty-five credits," the robot replied.

Raia pulled the bag out from her bra, counted out the credits, and dropped them into the payment compartment. She should have known better than to make a bet with these two furry connivers. She never won.

"You two are going to bankrupt me," she muttered, stuffing the bag of credits back into her bra.

The delighted snorts were barely smothered when she removed her jacket and dropped it on top of the two gloating creatures nestled inside her backpack. She lay her hand back on her blaster just as the three figures came to a stop in front of her.

"Can I help you?" she casually asked.

The person in front stepped closer to her table while the other two remained a few feet away, studying the surrounding crowd. There was something off about the group. They were dressed like Chazen Desert Dwellers, but the goggles were wrong.

"Beza ja milla en chew EA?" 'Are you the one who commands the EA?' the woman asked.

"Yes, I'm the captain of the Explorer Adventure II," she replied, fingering her glass of liquor. "I'll ask you again. How can I help you?"

The woman slid into the seat across from her. The shorter of the woman's two companions pulled up a chair and sat beside her. The other man walked over and leaned against the nearest support post. Although he wasn't standing near the table and wasn't an active part of the conversation, she knew he was listening as he surveilled the crowd.

She raised an eyebrow and examined the two sitting at the table with her. They all remained silent as the robot brought the fruit platter and cream that she had requested. Raia finally spoke once the robot had moved on to another customer.

"So… are you going to tell me who you really are? The whole Chazen Desert Dweller get-up needs some serious work. Your accent was pretty good though," she added.

The woman sighed as she reached up and removed her goggles. Raia stiffened with surprise when she saw the distinctive purple skin revealed underneath. The last thing she needed was to get mixed up with the Marastin Dow. She had been avoiding them—and a lot of other people—over the last ten years.

"Our business is finished," Raia growled, sitting forward.

"Please… hear us out," the woman softly pleaded.

Raia scowled. "Give me one good reason why I should," she demanded.

"Ander Ray," the woman said.

Raia jerked back in her seat in surprise. Her scowl deepened as she studied the woman's face—or at least what she could see of it. Anger filled her, and she caressed the safety release on the blaster with her thumb.

"Ander is dead," she stated in a tone devoid of emotion.

"What if he isn't?" the man next to the woman said.

Raia looked at him. She couldn't see anything but her own reflection in his goggles. She tapped the barrel of her blaster with her index finger. The silence grew. She sat back and waited.

"Are you suggesting that Ander could still be alive?" she quietly asked.

The woman paused before she spoke. "We've heard rumors. My name is Mieka Reddick. My two companions are Taylah Marks... and Marus Tylis," she introduced.

Raia raised an eyebrow. "Is that supposed to mean something to me?" she demanded.

Mieka sighed and shook her head. "No, but perhaps the name Berman De'Mar might," she replied.

Raia shook her head. "Nope, never heard of him," she retorted.

"This is a waste of our time," Marus Tylis snapped.

Mieka turned to the man and shook her head. "Marus, she may very well be our last hope," she quietly responded.

"Well, this is definitely your last chance to convince me to stick around and listen to you," Raia dryly commented.

"Berman De'Mar was a friend of Ander Ray," Taylah Marks stated.

Raia scoffed. "What does this have to do with me? Ander was murdered by the Marastin Dow fourteen years ago. If you think trying to convince me that he may still be alive will persuade me to work with you guys, you can think again. I've only met two Marastin Dow in my life that I would give two credits for, and neither one of them is sitting at this table," she snapped.

"Please, hear me out," Mieka begged with an edge in her voice.

Raia's jacket moved as if on its own.

"What in the—" Marus exclaimed.

Raia bit back a groan when Chummy's tiny paws peeked out. A split second later, Pi appeared on the table. Pi grinned at the startled faces around her before filling her mouth and arms with as much fruit as she could and vanished as quickly as she had appeared.

Raia should have known her two companions wouldn't be able to resist the smell of the fresh fruit and creamy, flavored milk. She barely grabbed the cup of milk before Chummy pulled it off the table. She picked it up and slid it under her jacket into her backpack. She knew if she didn't, Pi would reappear to get it. The last thing she needed right now was for her two friends to be seen by some cutthroat looking to make a fast credit on the black market.

And... it looks like my bag is going to need another good cleaning tonight, she silently grimaced at the noisy slurping sounds coming from the interior.

"They are one of the reasons why she is perfect for this mission," Mieka replied.

"What mission?" Raia warily asked.

"We will pay you one hundred thousand credits to break into the Spardonian Prison and rescue a prisoner," Mieka replied in a low tone.

Raia stared blankly at the woman sitting across from her. She must have misunderstood her. Had the woman just asked her to break into a Marastin Dow prison—and release a prisoner—for one hundred thousand credits?

She blinked and shook her head. "You want me to do what?" she asked in an incredulous tone.

"We want you to rescue General Behr De'Mar from the Spardonian Prison where he is being held. The Marastin High Council plans to execute him in less than three days. Can you do it?" Marus demanded.

Raia shook her head again in disbelief. "Why do you want me to break him out? Aren't you guys always trying to kill each other? Wouldn't it make more sense just to let the Council do it and save you the time, hassle, and mess?" she suggested.

"We don't want him dead! We need him alive. Do you want the job or not?" Taylah asked in a harsh tone.

Mieka reached across the table as if to touch her arm. Raia jerked her arm away and sat back. Mieka drew back and studied her with a thoughtful but determined expression.

"Do you know Hanine and Evetta Marquette and their human mates?" Mieka inquired in a low voice.

Raia's eyes narrowed. "So help me, if any of you have harmed one hair on their heads I'll put a hole through each one of you," she threatened.

Mieka shook her head in exasperation. "They are fine. They are… helping us as much as they can. You left a book with them. A book from your world," Mieka shared.

Raia blinked in surprise. "Yeah, so what?" she retorted.

"The book, and Ben and Aaron's translation of it into our language, has been invaluable to our cause. Have you read it?" Mieka asked.

Raia shrugged. "A few times," she replied, purposely remaining vague until she understood exactly where the conversation was going.

"The book is very important, but it is only one component for my people. We need a strong leader. Behr is that leader. Did… Ander give you anything else with the book?" Mieka inquired.

"No," Raia answered, looking the other woman in the eye. "Why? What are you looking for?"

Mieka sat back and glanced at the two men on either side of her before returning her attention to Raia, who could tell the other woman was holding something back. What it was, she didn't know.

She was about to press the other woman when she felt Pi's tiny fingers on her arm. Visions of them inside what was obviously a secure military installation filled her mind. She glimpsed the image of a man sitting on the edge of a cot with his head bowed.

I can't spend a hundred thousand credits if I'm dead, she silently pointed out.

We help man, Chummy said, adding to Pi's vision.

Raia pulled her arm free of Pi's grasp and glared back at the woman. "I want fifty percent up front. I pick the rendezvous location. You'll get that information after I have broken your man out and we are on our way," she stated.

"How do you plan to get him out?" Taylah asked.

Raia shook her head. "What I do and how I do it aren't part of the discussion," she said.

"How do we know you won't just take off with the credits?" Marus harshly demanded.

Raia looked at him. "I didn't come looking for you. You came looking for me. Do we have a deal or not?" she snapped.

"We have a deal. Here is our contact information and the credits," Mieka said, withdrawing a pouch and sliding it across the table.

Raia took the bag, slid it under the table, and quickly counted it out. She placed the pouch inside her backpack and sent a mental note to Chummy and Pi to transport the pouch to the ship. There was no way she wanted to walk around a Spaceport with that amount of credits on her.

"I'll contact you once I have your man and set up the location for the exchange," Raia said.

"Very well. Remember, you have less than three days before General Behr is to be executed," Mieka reminded her as she stood.

"I know, I know," Raia said with a casual wave of her hand.

Raia waited until the three Marastin Dow officers left the bar before she picked up her drink and took a sip. She barely hid her grimace of distaste. She hated alcohol. The only reason she had ordered it was to fit in. The drink was the only one she ever remembered Ander drinking, though she couldn't fathom why. The mixture of liquor created a chemical reaction that caused steam to rise from it. Ander once told her that ice could cause it to boil and burn your throat going down. Why anyone would want something that could scorch them from the inside out was beyond her!

Shaking her head, she placed the drink on the table, reached into her pack, removed the now empty cup of milk, and dropped in the few remaining pieces of uneaten fruit for later. Sliding on her jacket, she gathered her belongings and exited the bar, keeping a wary eye out for anyone who might be following her.

"Do you really think she can break him out without getting them both killed?" Marus asked, watching from the shadows as Raia exited the bar.

"Yes, I do," Mieka replied with a slight smile.

"I would love to know how she plans on doing it," Taylah murmured.

"So would I," Marus replied, wishing he felt as confident as Mieka.

CHAPTER TWO

Spardonian Prison Complex
Marastin Dow Home World

"This is not my best idea," Raia muttered under her breath.

"Triavarian Trader 519, you are cleared for landing in Bay 8," the landing tech stated.

"Triavarian Trader 519 acknowledges clearance for Bay 8," Raia replied.

She steered the dilapidated trading shuttle to the designated landing bay, engaged the landing gear, and gently nestled the shuttle within the hexagon-shaped landing cube. One advantage of being on a planet where everyone wanted to kill each other was that they were extremely paranoid. Even the traders were wary of being a target.

The few traders who would do business with the Marastin Dow insisted on security for their ships, even if the Marastin Dow couldn't guarantee the traders' personal safety once they left it. Each landing bay was hexagon shaped, a small part of a large honeycomb. Each trader was given a specific bay. Once they arrived, they controlled the security code for entry and exit.

"Triavarian Trader 519, prepare for security clearance and cargo check," the landing bay tech instructed.

"MDSC 1, Triavarian Trader 519 requesting permission for Hazards Team. I have a load of Tirrella power crystals setting off alarms. I would like to get the damn containers off my ship before they are opened," Raia replied.

For good measure, she activated the radiation alarm. The computer's automated voice warning about a spike in temperature, radiation threat, and possible imminent explosion echoed through the bridge. She broadly grinned when she heard the tech muttering a curse.

"Or, if you'd like to bypass the paperwork, I could pull the load off and reseal the crystals myself before delivery. I have the equipment. I just need to unload the containers so I can isolate the malfunctioning one," she suggested.

A brief silence greeted her request. She sat back and examined her fingernails as she waited. She knew what was happening—the tech was talking to his immediate supervisor. A glance at the time told her that the shift change would be occurring in less than half-an-hour.

If the current staff didn't agree with her request, it would mean a very long night for them. The next shift wouldn't want to deal with the paperwork and headaches involved with the Hazmat Team. They certainly would have no desire to deal with a load of unstable Tirrella power crystals.

"Can you stabilize the delivery?" the tech asked.

Raia grinned. "Yeah, I just need to move the items around to re-stabilize the load," she replied.

"Stabilize the load and deliver per your schedule to E5," the tech ordered.

"Acknowledged: stabilize and deliver to E5," she repeated.

She ended the link and shut off the alarm. Reaching up, she adjusted the digital voice box pressed against her larynx and double-checked the disguise she was wearing.

Thanks to Hanine and Evetta, she wasn't the only one in disguise. The EA II looked like a derelict shuttle transport instead of a mint-condition freighter. The hologram disks mounted to the outer hull allowed her to change the appearance of her ship.

She used the ability to disguise her ship to slip in and out of different air spaces undetected. Her favorite was the ability to make the ship virtually invisible. Hanine was still working on a way to cover the ion trail left by the engines. So far, the only thing the two sisters came up with was discharging decoy rocket canisters.

"Pi, you're up," she called.

Pi rolled down the corridor toward her and unfurled. Raia bent down and affectionately scratched her furry friend behind the ear. She always worried when the little Marica Peekaboo went out on her own. She reminded herself that Pi was the most likely one out of the three of them to escape practically any situation.

"Remember, you need to find this room," she said, kneeling and showing Pi the location on the map.

Pi tilted her head and studied the map before she pointed to a star in the corner. Raia nodded. Pi grinned at her, wiggled her nose in acknowledgement, and vanished.

"Okay, Chummy. It's show time," she said.

She opened the bag draped across her body. Chummy scrambled in and peeked out of the top. She handed him a piece of fruit, scratched the top of his head, and lowered the flap.

Striding down the corridor, she headed for the storage bay. She tapped the remote on her wrist and the bay platform opened. She had loaded a cargo skid earlier with a cunningly designed container marked with a Tirrella power crystal warning. The top opened to reveal a layer of crystals, but underneath that layer it was a different matter.

"Here we go," she mumbled.

She guided the cargo skid down the ramp and closed the platform. She purposely stopped the skid under the surveillance camera. From this view, the tech could see the flashing warning light she had rigged on the container.

She opened the top, revealing the layer of power crystals, then knelt beside the container and removed the control panel. Several minutes passed as she maintained the illusion of working on the defective container before she switched off the alarms, rose, and resealed the container. She looked up at the camera.

"Secure your bay and proceed to E5," the tech instructed.

She raised her hand in acknowledgement. Guiding the cargo skid over to the bay door, she placed a portable control module over the existing one. Thin connectors integrated with the existing locking device, overriding it.

Not that she didn't trust the Marastin Dow's promise of independent security for each bay, but—she didn't. There was no way in hell she was going to trust her ship anywhere near them—or half the other inhabitants in the galaxy. She followed the map Evetta had reluctantly given her.

"The map is old. It may not be relevant any longer. I don't want to ask why you need a map for such a place!"

Relevant or not, it would have to do.

"Which way?" she muttered.

Pi say go this way, Chummy silently instructed.

Raia glanced down and saw Chummy sticking one paw out of the bag, pointing to the left. The connection between Pi and Chummy had grown as they matured. They were almost always connected no matter how far apart they were, while her connection with both creatures still relied on being close, if not touching.

Raia turned to the left, and a group of seven or eight Marastin Dow warriors walked by her. Her heart thumped heavily in her chest. They sneered at her as they passed.

Well, I definitely picked the right disguise, she thought.

The Dregulon holographic image surrounding her made her look two feet taller than she was, two hundred pounds heavier, and ugly enough to keep even the amorous Triloug she dealt with at the bar a few days ago from approaching her. She also chose the male version, which required the use of a voice adaptor.

"This is what happens when you spend too much time in the Tirrella mines," one of the warriors quipped.

"Don't get too close. You don't know how radioactive he is," a female warrior advised.

Raia ignored the group as they moved away. She hadn't considered that she might be viewed as a potential danger. That might work to her advantage.

"Chummy, where is Pi?" she asked.

No sooner did the words leave her mouth than she saw her furry friend. Pi was in the control room up ahead. One way led to Engineering Maintenance and the other way led to the prison cells where she needed to go.

Pi was sitting on top of a series of cabinets. There were two men inside the control room. Raia turned to the left instead of the right when she reached the intersection.

One of the men frowned and motioned to her. She acted like she didn't see him and continued along the corridor. The man reached out and knocked on the glass. Raia continued to act like she didn't hear him.

Out of the corner of her eye, she saw the two men talking before the one who had banged on the glass opened the door and stepped out. She was forced to stop when he stood in her path. Grumbling under her breath, she glared at the man.

"I've got a load of Tirrella power crystals to deliver," she snapped.

"You are going the wrong way. This is the prisoner cell block. You need to go to the right," the man informed her.

"The map the tech gave me said to go to the left," she growled.

"The map is wrong. Engineering Maintenance is to the right," the man retorted with annoyance.

"Stupid Tech. He probably wasted my time on purpose," she grumbled.

"I'll speak with his supervisor in the morning," the man replied.

She shifted from one foot to the other. In order for her plan to work, she needed to get both men out of the control room. Maneuvering the cargo skid, she almost rammed the man standing in the corridor.

"Watch what you're doing!" he snapped, barely jumping out of the way.

"The controller is acting up," she said.

She slapped the controller against her palm. The skid swung back around, nearly running over the man and slamming into the wall across from the door. She mumbled an apology when the man angrily yelled at her again.

Just as she had hoped, the second guard stepped out of the room to see what was going on. Raia pressed the button on the side of the controller and started the container alarm as Pi quietly closed and locked the door to the control room behind the second man.

"What's going on?" the second guard demanded.

"The container is malfunctioning, and the crystals are overheating again," she stated.

A second alarm sounded. "Warning: Radiation levels rising to dangerous level. Power crystal destabilization detected. Warning," a computerized voice stated.

"What the… get that thing out of here!" the first guard demanded.

Raia shook her head. "I can't move it until I've stabilized the container. If I do, it could explode," she replied.

"Well, fix it!" the second guard ordered, retreating until his back was pressed against the locked door.

"Warning: Radiation levels are reaching critical levels," the computer stated.

Raia pushed a second button, and a loud hissing cloud of glowing red fog began to seep out from under the lid. She hid her grin when both men turned and tried to get back into the control room. They frantically waved their badges in front of the door control.

"Being in there won't save you from radiation. You've got to be in a fully enclosed room farther away," she stated.

"How far?" the first guard demanded.

She looked at the end of the corridor and nodded. "One of those little cells would work. Well, would you look at that! My skin is beginning to burn," she commented, holding up a holographic hand that was beginning to blister. "Radiation must be bad enough to burn your bollocks if I'm turning toasty," she reflected.

"Move out of the way," the second guard growled, pushing the first one to the side.

"Wait for me," the first guard called.

Now, Chummy, she instructed.

Chummy peeked out from the bag and focused on the security badges attached to the men's waists. He pulled the badges off seconds before they stepped into the cell. Pi appeared in midair, captured the cards and flashed one across the access panel, locking the two men in the cell.

Raia watched as her furry friend curled into a ball and rolled back toward them. Bending down, she plucked one of the badges out of Pi's outstretched hands and turned off the alarm on the container. She jerked her head toward the door.

"Can you unlock it for me?" she requested.

Pi grinned and disappeared. Seconds later, the door opened, and Raia stepped inside. On the row of monitors, she could see inside each cell. She grinned at the two guards who were pacing back and forth in the cell. She didn't miss the way they both kept touching their balls to make sure they were still there.

"Well, hello, General De'Mar. I think today is your lucky day," she said.

Her target was sitting on the edge of his cot with his head bowed, his arms on his knees, and his hands clasped together thanks to the wrist cuffs he was wearing. All she could see was the top of his head. She estimated he was around six feet tall.

"It's going to be a tight fit. I hope the guy is flexible," she muttered. "Pi, he's in the cell at the end of the corridor. You take your badge and unlock his wrist cuffs. We aren't going to have much time before someone figures out that something hinky is going on."

Behr De'Mar worked the small piece of metal he had finally broken free from the cot into the seam where the wrist cuffs locked. It would take a miracle to break free of the cuffs and an even larger one for him to escape the cell and make it out of this prison alive. He grimly acknowledged that this time he might not be so lucky.

"Sheetz ta!" 'Shit!' he muttered when the wire slipped and cut his finger.

He studied the blood beading from the wound. Rolling his shoulders to ease his tension, he closed his eyes. The weight of exhaustion pounding at him was bone deep. He couldn't remember the last time he had a full night's rest.

General Maradash and the Council members had made sure of that. When the drugs hadn't worked on him, they resorted to sleep deprivation to lower his resistance. They wanted the locations of the rebel bases and their fleet positions, along with intel on those supporting the revolution against the tyranny of the Council, but so far, Behr had refused to give them anything.

He was guaranteed a painful death. Maradash had informed him that he was to receive a ritual public execution modeled after the ancient ways of the Marastin Dow which is one reason he had been kept in relatively good health. No one wanted to watch a half-dead man put to death. It was always more fun to cheer on one still alive and kicking. If he were lucky, he would die from the death of a thousand cuts. If not, he would feel the excruciating pain of slowly being roasted alive.

Nothing says civilized like being tortured and murdered while everyone watches, he grimly thought, opening his eyes.

Another curse burst from his lips when the piece of metal slipped again and cut the palm of his hand. At the rate he was going, he might finish the job for Maradash before he arrived. Shaking his head at the morbid thought, he twisted and wiped the blood on the hard surface of the cot. He would never give Maradash or the Council the pleasure of hearing him beg for mercy—nor betray everything that he and others had lived and died for over the past twenty years.

"May the Goddesses keep our hearts true and our cause strong," he murmured, closing his eyes and bowing his head.

It would be so easy to accept his fate and fall asleep. He felt no remorse at his decisions. Maradash commenting that he was weak like his father had actually had the opposite effect on him. He knew his father had been strong. Berman De'Mar was a Marastin Dow ahead of his time who believed there was a better way of life for their people than the constant threat of death from their own. His father had shared that hope with him—and many others.

Behr lifted his cuffed hands and rubbed his brow. His father had been searching for something when he disappeared. The only thing he knew was that it had something to do with the Marastin Dow doctrines said to have been lost centuries ago. Behr didn't know if the doctrines were myth or real. All he knew was that his father had believed in them enough to spend his life searching for them.

He sighed, lowered his hands, and opened his eyes. He jumped to his feet when a tan and white creature suddenly appeared in front of him. The creature grinned and sat up. Behr gaped in shock when the creature held up a thin badge in one tiny hand.

"What in the…! Where did you come from?" he hissed.

His surprise doubled when the door to his cell suddenly opened, and he found himself face-to-face with a Dregulon. The Dregulon stared back at him in silence. He shook his head, wondering if he was hallucinating.

"This cell is taken," he dryly commented.

The Dregulon blinked as if coming out of a trance before responding, "Not for long. Pi, unlock his wrist cuffs."

The small tan and white creature climbed up his leg and tugged on his sleeve. Behr held his wrists out so the creature could unlock the cuffs. He rubbed his wrists after the cuffs fell to the floor with a loud clang, and warily studied the man standing in the doorway.

"Well, do you want to get out of here or not? I have fifty thousand credits riding on this," the man snapped.

"How do you propose getting me through the prison complex undetected?" he asked.

The Dregulon smiled. "That depends on how good you are at being a contortionist," the man replied.

Behr warily stepped forward when the man turned away. He paused at the entrance to his cell and looked down the corridor. It was empty except for a large cargo skid stacked with a series of containers marked with the warning symbol of Tirrella power crystals.

"Where are the guards?" he asked.

The Dregulon paused lifting the lid off the top container and grinned. "They are locked in a cell, feeling their balls, hoping they don't shrivel and fall off."

Behr stepped out of his cell and eyed the container. "There is no way I will fit in there," he stated.

The man eyed him up and down. "You won't be comfortable, but you'll fit," the Dregulon firmly replied.

Behr stepped aside when the man pulled a tray of Tirrella power crystals out of the container and walked into the cell. The man placed the tray on the cot along with something that looked suspiciously like a detonator. He moved aside again when the man walked by him.

"Climb in," the man instructed with a wave of his hand.

Behr peered into the container. He was surprised to see that it appeared to be a stack of four short containers but was actually one large container. At the bottom lay a blaster. This seemed to be the rescue he needed, but still, he hesitated.

"Listen, we don't have all day," the man grumbled.

"Who sent you?" he demanded.

The man muttered a curse. "Surprisingly, some Marastin Dow who didn't want you dead."

Behr didn't move.

"Mieka, Marus, and Taylah if that helps," the man added.

Shock and relief swept through him. Without another word, he stepped up onto the skid and climbed over the side into the container. He bent over and picked up the laser pistol before he squatted. His knees were almost touching his chin by the time he positioned himself as far down as he could go.

"You may have to bend your head down," the man advised. "Good thing I wasn't planning on using the tray of crystals," the Dregulon muttered to himself.

"I hope you know what you're doing," Behr gritted out in a low voice.

"Sit tight. We've got this," the man cheerfully replied.

Behr wasn't sure if the man was being sarcastic or not. Whatever the case, he wasn't going to argue with a miracle even if it came in the form of a Dregulon with a bad sense of humor. He rested his forehead on his knees and closed his eyes when darkness surrounded him. It would be so easy to close his eyes and fall asleep, but he feared that if he did, he would wake up and this would all have been a dream.

CHAPTER THREE

Raia guided the cargo skid back down the corridor. At the intersection, she retraced her steps. She was almost to the end when a lift opened and a large group of Marastin Dow personnel stepped out. Her heart sank when she saw the man in the lead.

The black uniform distinguished him as a high-ranking member of the military. A shiver ran through her when she saw the coldness in the man's eyes and recognized him from her research—Field General Reynar Maradash. He was a man who enjoyed causing pain and suffering to others. His presence caused a far different experience than what had held her in stunned silence when she first gazed into Behr De'Mar's eyes.

Raia halted the skid as close to the wall as it would go and pressed her back against the cold, hard surface. She instinctively moved her hand to the bag draped across her body as the man came closer. She kept her eyes averted in a non-challenging manner.

"General Maradash, the Council wants to be in attendance for the execution," the female Council Liaison reminded him in a forceful tone.

"I'm well aware of the Council's expectations," Maradash coolly replied.

"They are not expecting the execution until tomorrow," the woman continued in a more moderate voice.

Raia bit the inside of her cheek to keep from saying anything. If the woman was stupid enough to keep talking, that was on her head. It was obvious from where Raia stood that Maradash didn't give a damn about what anyone wanted—including the Marastin Dow Council members. Unease filled Raia when Maradash stopped less than three feet away from her.

"Lieutenant Jaten," Maradash said as he turned and looked at a woman standing behind the Council Liaison.

"Yes, General Maradash," Jaten responded, standing at attention.

"I'm promoting you to Council Liaison," he stated in a bone-chilling voice.

"Th-thank you, sir," Jaten answered in a hesitant manner as she warily stared at the woman in front of her.

Raia stood frozen, watching in horror as the General rotated on his heel, pulled out a foot-long blade, and slid it between the former Council Liaison's ribs. The woman's eyes widened in shock. Her cry of pain was muffled by General Maradash's hand covering her mouth.

"Your services are no longer required," he murmured indifferently.

No one stepped forward to catch the woman when Maradash withdrew the knife and her knees buckled. He held the blade out to Jaten. The woman gingerly took the handle, holding it away from her body.

"Have that cleaned and returned to me," he ordered.

"Yes, sir," Jaten quavered.

Raia stiffened when Maradash's gaze locked on her. Sweat beaded on her brow as he continued to stare at her in silence. She forced her hand to remain on the outside of her bag. The last thing she wanted was for him to think she was going for a weapon.

"Clean up this mess," he ordered before he turned away and continued down the corridor.

Raia waited until the group reached the end of the corridor and turned out of view before she made a decision that she hoped she wouldn't regret. Opening the lid of the container, she peered over the edge at Behr. He stared back up at her, his eyes narrowed against the sudden brightness.

"Change of plans, General," she said.

"Chummy, I need Hanine's popper," she instructed.

Chummy groaned. Raia felt like groaning along with him. She had only used Hanine's portable transporter once before, and the resultant after-effects weren't pleasant. The process had left her nauseated and with a lingering case of vertigo that took weeks to fade. She had brought it along as a last resort.

"What…? Maradash— I would recognize his work anywhere," he grimly remarked as he stared down at the deceased woman lying in a pool of her own blood.

"Yeah. I don't want to be here when he discovers you're missing," she said.

He climbed over the top of the container. "You should have brought more than one laser pistol. Where in the hell did Mieka find you?" he snapped.

Raia glared at Behr. "In a bar. Where else would they find someone crazy enough to bust out a Marastin Dow General from a Marastin Dow Prison on the Marastin Dow home world?" she sarcastically retorted.

"A bar," he repeated doubtfully. "What *exactly* is your expertise?" he asked.

"Blowing things up and disappearing," she replied, grabbing his arm and activating the transporter device as the Tirrella power crystals she had placed in his cell detonated in a fiery blast.

Behr swayed. He reached out and steadied himself with a hand against the wall. It took a few seconds for his brain to catch up with what his eyes were seeing. They were no longer in the prison corridor. From the interior, he would guess they were inside a freighter.

He scanned the area, turned to face the Dregulon, and did a double-take, wondering if he was hallucinating. Stunned disbelief held him frozen. Instead of the ugly male, a beautifully exotic woman stood beside him with her eyes closed. She was breathing deeply, while keeping one hand pressed against her stomach. After a few seconds, she opened her almond-shaped, dark-brown eyes and looked back at him with a wry smile.

"So far, so good," she said in the Dregulon's deep voice.

She made a face, reached up, and removed a thin patch pressed against her throat. He followed the movement with his eyes, fascinated by her slender fingers. She gripped the strap of her bag and pulled it over her head.

"Time to go," she said in her normal, slightly husky feminine voice.

All he could do was nod. He stepped aside as she pushed past him and strode across the bay to a corridor entrance. He followed her, his brain still trying to assimilate what he was seeing.

"Who *are* you?" he demanded, following her.

"Captain Raia of the *Explorer's Adventure II*, at your service," she replied, flashing him a crooked grin over her shoulder.

She paused by a door and lowered the bag in her hand. Two furry creatures scrambled out of it and into the room. She glanced at him again before she headed farther down the corridor toward the freighter's cockpit.

He passed the room she had stopped in front of, looking inside. The two creatures had scrambled up onto a table where a basket of fruit sat. The tan and white one looked at him with a wide grin while the spotted black and white one merely stared back at him with soft, dark eyes. He shook his head, wondering if he was going crazy when he heard a voice whisper *we keep him, too,* inside his mind.

"Hey, General, do you want to get out of here or not? If that blast didn't kill Maradash, he is going to be pissed as hell. Personally, I don't want to be here if he survived," the woman called.

Behr turned toward the front of the ship and strode down the corridor. The alarms outside were muted by the ship's hull, but he could see the flashing red emergency lights through the front glass. The ship's deck rumbled under his feet as the woman powered it up. He climbed the steps and slid into the co-pilot seat.

"Is there anyone else on board this ship?" he asked.

She shook her head as her hands flitted across the controls with a sureness that spoke of long experience. She pulled up a navigation screen and tapped a spot on it before sweeping it away with a swipe of her hand.

"Triavarian Trader 519, you are not cleared for lift off. Power down your space craft," the bay tech ordered.

"Not likely," she murmured. "You might want to hang on to something. This might get a little bumpy," she suggested.

Behr gripped the armrests as the freighter lifted off. His attention moved to the airspace above them. A lattice-work of energy beams formed a dome over the bay.

"Watch out, they've activated a restraint shield," he warned.

"I've got this," she stated calmly.

She pulled up another screen. A diagram appeared depicting the bay's controls. She disabled the restraint shield for all bays. As they rose through the opening, Behr could see dozens of ships also lifting off. Smoke billowed from the prison section where the woman had set off the Tirrella power crystals. The roof over that cell block had collapsed.

"What are you going to do now?" he asked, fascinated by everything the woman had accomplished so far.

"We're going to get lost in the crowd," she said.

"General Maradash, are you hurt?" a medic asked.

Reynar Maradash stiffly rose from the floor. Around him, small fires continued to burn. The air was thick with smoke and debris particles. The bodies of his entourage lay scattered like broken twigs after a fierce storm.

He pushed the medic aside as he surveyed the damage. He would have died with them if he hadn't stepped into the control room a split second before the explosion. He had been protected by a tall cabinet that fell during the blast. Even so, he could feel a burning pain on the side of his face that had been pressed against the overheated metal.

"Where are the guards that were in charge of this prison corridor?" he demanded.

"We found them in one of the cells further down. One is dead, the other is wounded but still alive," the medic replied.

"Take me to him," Reynar ordered.

"This way, sir," the medic said.

Reynar waved off the man's hand when he reached to assist him over a section of debris. He paused when he saw a pale purple hand sticking out from under a section of the collapsed ceiling. Stiff, pale purple fingers were loosely wrapped around the hilt of a blood-stained blade.

He bent over and retrieved the blade, wiping the blood off with the dead woman's sleeve.

When he straightened, the medic stood in expressionless silence, watching and waiting for the General. Reynar stepped down off the fallen section of the rubble and walked over to a stretcher where the injured guard lay. Another medic was talking to the man.

Reynar stopped next to the stretcher. The man had a large gash across his forehead and from the odd angle of his right arm, he could see that it was broken. The guard paled when he looked up.

"Sir…," the guard greeted as he tried to sit up.

"What happened to De'Mar?" Reynar demanded.

The guard paled and swayed. The medic reached out and steadied him so he wouldn't fall off the gurney. The guard shook his head.

"I-I don't know. There was a Dregulon. He had a container full of Tirrella power crystals. The alarms went off and radiation started pouring out of it. He-he was trying to stabilize it. I guess the poor bastard didn't make it," the guard explained.

A vision of the Dregulon standing in the corridor flashed through Reynar's mind. He turned to gaze at the destruction at the end of the long corridor. A crater the size of a troop transport showed the origin of the blast. He turned to one of the rescue team's security personnel.

"Find the Dregulon and lock down all departures from this installation. No one is to leave either by ground or air," he ordered. "No one!"

"Yes, sir," the security officer replied.

He tightened his grip around the hilt of his blade. He resisted the impulse to bury it in the guard's chest. There were still unanswered questions. If he discovered that the man had been negligent in his duties, the guard would be wishing he died in the blast alongside his comrade.

"I want De'Mar's body found," he said.

"Yes, sir," the security officer replied.

Reynar turned away and picked his way through the debris. If De'Mar had escaped, there would be hell to pay. He had spent years chasing the bastard only to have him slip through his fingers time after time. If it turned out that the Dregulon had helped De'Mar escape and was responsible for the subsequent explosion, he vowed he would hunt down every damn Dregulon in the galaxy until he found the man from the corridor.

CHAPTER FOUR

"Chummy, please tell me you and Pi didn't drink all the Muza cream," Raia called over her shoulder with a low groan.

She held a hand to her churning stomach and peered inside the cold unit, muttering a sigh of relief when she saw the familiar glass bottle. Reaching past the array of packaged foods she purchased from the Spaceport a few days earlier, she pulled out the half-full container.

"What is the matter?" Behr asked.

She straightened and looked at him. He took a step toward her when she swayed but stopped when she held up her hand. She shook her head and gave him a weak smile.

"I'll be okay. I thought I was going to make it through the transporter jump with no side effects this time, but apparently I was wrong," she muttered.

Behr tried not to grin at her miserable, irritated expression. He must not have done a good job, because she shot him a heated glare and turned away. She lifted the container of liquid and drank straight from it.

"You have a little bit running down your chin," he pointed out.

She released a loud burp and wiped her chin with the back of her hand. "Thanks," she replied.

"You're welcome," he said.

He leaned against the doorframe as she poured herself a cup of something that looked like hot tea, added the cream to it, then pulled out a small bowl and poured some of the cream into it. She took both over to the U-shaped booth and placed the bowl on the table. In seconds, both creatures were sitting on the table, lapping up the cream. Raia affectionately scratched each of the creatures before she slid onto the bench seat, leaned her head back, and closed her eyes.

"If you're hungry, there is food in the cold storage and some in the cabinets. My replicator isn't working at the moment, and I haven't gotten around to replacing it yet," she informed him.

"Thank you. I *am* hungry. It has been a while since I last ate," he replied.

He walked over to the storage unit. Opening a cabinet, he shook his head. Packages of cookies filled each shelf. He opened a second and a third cabinet. They were also lined with a variety of cookies.

It would appear I will be dining on cookies for the duration of my visit, he mused.

He pulled out a package of fruit-filled cookies, walked over, and sat down at the table. He didn't even have the package opened all the way before both creatures appeared in front of him, staring up at him with wide, attentive gazes. He pulled out two cookies and handed one to each creature.

"You'll never get rid of them now," Raia mused.

His gaze locked with hers. She was looking at him with an amused expression. It finally hit him who—or at least what—species she was.

"You're a human," he said in a voice tinged with mild surprise.

She lifted her cup of tea and bowed her head in agreement. "Two credits for being right," she said.

"I once had the pleasure of meeting two human brothers," he murmured.

"I know. They—and one hundred thousand credits—are one of the reasons you are on my ship," she replied.

He frowned. "You have met Ben and Aaron Cooper?" he asked.

She nodded. "It would appear the universe is a small place. I met Ben, Aaron, and their wives ten years ago," she softly replied.

"Hanine and Evetta," he said.

She looked at him and nodded. "Yes. Hanine and Evetta have helped me turn the *EA II* into one of the best freighters in the star system," she proudly shared.

"Why did you take on such a risky mission? I imagine that Ben and Aaron wouldn't be pleased that you did," he said.

She scoffed, leaned her head back against the cushioned seat backing, and stared up at the ceiling. She pursed her lips and released a deep sigh.

"No, they weren't pleased. Neither were Hanine and Evetta, but they figured I'd do it anyway. They were more agreeable once I told them it was you that I was busting out. They think highly of you," she added.

She lifted her head and looked at him. For a moment, he was lost in the depths of her dark brown eyes. The pull he felt was so strong that he found himself leaning forward.

More cookie.

He blinked and lurched back. His attention moved to the small creature staring up at him. It had one paw on his hand.

"Did… what… I thought I heard…," he muttered with a shake of his head.

"Let me guess, Chummy asked you for another cookie," she dryly inquired.

He looked at her and nodded. "Yes. What are they?" he asked in fascination.

"My friends," she replied before sliding out of the booth. "I need to go check the scanners. Pi says we're okay for now, but I would still be more comfortable maintaining a vigilant eye on our unwelcome visitors hanging around not too far from here. I bought some clothes for you, not that it will be much of a disguise with your skin. You can get cleaned up, get some rest, and change in the cabin across the hall."

"What about you? If you are unwell…," he said.

She held up the cup of tea. "I'm fine. If you need anything, I'll be on the bridge or you can ask Chummy or Pi. They understand a lot more than most people guess," she added.

Behr watched as Raia exited the room. There was so much more that he wanted to ask her. He handed another cookie to Chummy and Pi and sat back in his seat. Who was the mysterious Captain Raia of the *Explorer's Adventure II*?

"One thing is for sure, I plan on finding out," he murmured to his two furry companions.

Raia gently swiveled back and forth in the captain's chair and moodily stared out into space. She wasn't sure if the queasiness she experienced was from Hanine's transporter or her intense physical reaction to General Behr De'Mar. If she was honest with herself, the queasiness started before she even used Hanine's popper.

She tapped the rim of her cup with her finger and scowled. Nothing had prepared her for how to deal with a man like Behr. He was handsome with his dark wavy hair, smooth purple complexion, and rich brown eyes that were the color of that sweet stuff called chocolate that Aaron always liked to give her.

"For crying out loud, Raia! Since when do you think about a guy like that?" she muttered.

Over the years, there had been plenty of opportunities to mingle with the opposite sex if she had wanted. Thanks to Pi and Chummy, she had been spared from the jerks, as Ben and Aaron would call them, and thanks to Hanine and Evetta, she could handle the assholes of the galaxy. Still, she was surprised that the first thought in her head when she saw Behr hadn't been on how she was going to get them out alive, but how damn hot he was.

With a muttered curse, she pulled up the communication panel and tapped in the encrypted password. Almost immediately, a cheery face appeared on the holographic screen. It was Ben and Evetta's thirteen-year-old son, Bennie. She made a groaning sound like she was about to faint and fell back in her seat.

"What's up, Rai-Rai?" Bennie greeted.

"I'm having a heart attack! I can't believe you aren't off playing a video game," she replied with a good-natured grin.

Bennie made a face. "I'm grounded for a week," he glumly replied.

Raia rubbed her hands together with glee and sat forward with an expectant expression. "What'd you do this time?" she asked.

Bennie grinned. "I took Dad's skimmer out without telling him. I was doing good—" he said.

"Until...?" she pressed.

He held up his arm. Seeing the bone regenerator on it, she sat back and made a sympathetic face. This must have been the third time Bennie had broken his arm in the last four years.

"I hit a tree. Mom and Hanine might have to rebuild it," he ruefully confessed.

"Ouch, that must have hurt. Speaking of your mom, is she there?" Raia inquired.

"Yeah, she just came in. Dad and Aaron are still out in the fields," he said as he turned and called to his mom.

Seconds later, Evetta's relieved face filled the screen. "Thank the Goddess you are alright," she said.

Raia scoffed. "Of course I'm alright," she retorted.

Evetta pursed her lips and gave her the same look that she gave Bennie when he was driving her crazy. Raia sighed. Ben and Evetta had become the parents she had lost. Evetta's expression softened with concern.

"What's wrong? Were you… too late to save Behr?" Evetta asked.

Raia shook her head. "No, I got him out. I had to use Hanine's popper," she confessed.

"Are you alright? Did the biometric changes Hanine added help with your reactions?" Evetta asked.

"Yeah, they helped a lot. I had a little nausea, but I tried the tea and Muza cream like you suggested and it went away," Raia said.

"Something is bothering you. What is it?" Evetta asked.

Raia bit her lip. This was a conversation that she had avoided for several years and one that she wasn't looking forward to having now. She shifted uncomfortably in her seat before she finally looked back up at Evetta.

"How did you figure out that Ben was—you know—the guy for you?" she blurted out.

Evetta looked puzzled for a moment before her eyes widened and her lips parted in surprise. A slightly darker shade of purple suffused Evetta's cheeks, and she appeared to be a little unsure of what to say.

"The first time I saw Ben, I had just had a very traumatic altercation with a fellow crew member. Ben was playing his harmonica, and I was drawn to the sound. I'd never heard anything like it before—or seen anyone like him. I found him physically attractive, even though he was different from any other man I had ever met. But… it was more than that. I was fascinated by the way he treated me, talked to me…, and when he touched me—it was like my mind and body connected with him," she said with a faraway look in her eyes.

"That is pretty awesome," Raia softly replied.

Evetta blinked. "Why do you ask? Have you met someone?" she asked with an intense look that made Raia flush.

"No… at least… I'm not sure. It is too weird to talk about. Did it bother you… or Ben that you were different from each other?" she asked.

Evetta smiled and shook her head. "Do you mean because I am a Marastin Dow and he is human, or because our physical appearance is different from each other?" she asked.

"I don't know—both, I guess," Raia murmured.

"No. Ben didn't have the prejudices against the Marastin Dow that many do, which helped. But, I don't think it would have made much of a difference. There was something about him I couldn't resist, and he felt the same way about me," Evetta confessed.

"So, how were you sure Ben was the guy for you? Did you… like kiss him and see explosions?" Raia persisted in a frustrated voice.

Evetta laughed. "There might have been a few explosions when he kissed me. You'll know when it happens, Raia," she said with a confident smile.

"But... what if I feel something and... say hypothetically if there *was* someone... that the-the guy doesn't?" Raia mumbled, fidgeting with her cup.

The smile faded from Evetta's lips and was replaced with an expression of concern. "Have you dropped Behr at the rendezvous location yet?" she asked.

Raia shook her head. "There are too many Marastin Dow ships out at the moment. We are going to hang low for a few days and hope they leave. There's a place near our location where we can hide. It should be safe," she said.

"Whatever happens, Raia, don't get caught. The Marastin Dow have no limits to their brutality and General Maradash's form of cruelty is beyond anything we have ever witnessed before. No one—not even the Curizan, Sarafin, or Valdier—could save you, I fear," Evetta cautioned.

"Hey, careful is my middle name. Besides, Pi will warn me if trouble is coming," Raia said with confidence.

"I know you trust Pi, but it never hurts to be extra cautious," Evetta insisted.

"I promise to be extra careful. I've seen firsthand what Maradash can do," Raia replied.

"As much as we didn't want you to do this, Raia, we are also very thankful and proud of you. You have given hope to the Marastin Dow who are fighting for a better way of life," Evetta said.

Tears burned Raia's eyes at the emotion in Evetta's voice. Thanks to her extended family, she was aware of the Marastin Dow's rebellion and the dangers to those who wanted a different way of life. She also knew how cruel those that didn't want the change could be.

"I love you, Evetta. I'll check in again in a few days," she promised.

"We love you, too, Raia. Stay safe," Evetta said.

Raia closed the communication hologram and sat back in her seat. Her focus moved to the glow of lights from the large warships moving in the distance. She had activated the hologram disks attached to the outside of the *EA II*, adjusting them to reflect the surrounding space. She had also cut all power to the engines. The only thing running was environmental.

She had piggy-backed on the communication channels of ships within range to hide her transmission. It helped that Hanine had encrypted the signal so that everything came out sounding like normal chatter between freight captains. Of course, nothing would sound out of the ordinary—well, mostly nothing as long as it wasn't something like a hoard of Marastin Dow boarding your freighter.

Where's the Curizan military when you need it? she thought with a sigh.

CHAPTER FIVE

Reynar pushed the melted remains of the electronic box away and rose from his seat. A cold rage built inside him as he walked over to the window overlooking the prison. The destroyed cell block was clearly visible, even in the dark, thanks to all the construction lights illuminating the shambles caused by the blast.

The report he just finished reading confirmed his suspicions—Behr De'Mar had escaped. Video surveillance supported the surviving guard's statement. The Dregulon, along with two unusual creatures, were responsible.

What infuriated him the most was that, at one point, De'Mar had been mere feet from him. The video cut out after the explosion. The only other information was images of the dilapidated freighter from Bay 8 and the melted remains of the device attached to the computerized locking panel.

There was a brief knock before the door opened. He turned and waited as his newest assistant introduced the three guests he had requested. He waved his hand in dismissal. His assistant bowed his head and closed the door.

"General Maradash," the woman coolly greeted.

"Akita," he replied with a nod before he turned his attention to the two men standing beside her.

"From the looks of the damage, someone kicked your ass," He'lo proffered as a greeting.

He'lo carefully scrutinized his damaged face. The scarred skin on Reynar's cheek tightened and pulled when he pursed his lips. It was obvious that the assassin was referring to his wound rather than the damage to the prison that was visible through the glass behind him. As much as Reynar detested working with these three assassins, they would be a necessity.

"I have an assignment. The first one to deliver will receive two million credits," he stated.

"What is the target?" Orb asked.

Reynar turned to the short, stocky assassin. The man's flattish snout twitched while he flexed his wide mouth—causing the twin tusks protruding from his lower jaw to move up and down. Layers of ridges along his cheeks, rising to his forehead, were marred with scars from previous battles. Orb's black, beady eyes looked like two pieces of polished obsidian—a match for his name.

"A prisoner escaped. I want him and the Dregulon who broke him free found and returned to me alive," he ordered.

"Alive? That will cost you extra. It is always harder to bring them in alive. They tend to fight," Akita drawled.

Akita was one of the rare Marastin Dow warriors born with a deeper purple complexion and a shock of white hair. The milky glow of her red eyes was deceptive. Many would have assumed her blind. Her own parents had, so they gave her to the Marastin Dow researchers who replaced her retinas with ones that could read heat signatures.

"I want them alive," he reiterated.

"Akita's correct, bringing them in alive is difficult. It is also more dangerous—for us. Men about to die are a little more passionate about escaping," He'lo replied, folding his massive arms.

Reynar glared back at the Triloug. The man's two tails moved in sync. Through the opening of He'lo's shirt, Reynar noted a fresh scar across the man's bright yellow chest plate. The wound had to have been deep to penetrate the thick scales that protected the Triloug's vital organs underneath.

"I don't care how you do it. You'll only get half of the credits if either of them are dead," he retorted.

"Do these targets have a name? Images would help," Akita added.

Reynar walked over to his desk and picked up three information disks. He held one out to Akita before handing the other two to the male assassins. He pursed his lips, which pulled on the wound to his face again, when Akita's attention returned to his ravaged cheek.

"They are most likely still together. The first man is a Marastin Dow. His name is Behr De'Mar. You'll find all the information you need, including his images, on the disk. The second man is an unknown Dregulon. They are traveling together. We've been unable to locate his freighter—yet. The identification number given to us belonged to an obsolete freighter that was scrapped six months ago," he stated.

"Behr De'Mar...," Akita murmured with a purr.

Reynar's eyes narrowed at the amused note in Akita's voice when she said De'Mar's name. She returned his glare with a raised eyebrow and cold eyes. He studied her face for a moment longer before he spoke.

"What about the two furry creatures? Are they part of the package?" Orb asked.

Reynar waved a dismissive hand. "You can kill them. I have no use for the creatures," he said.

"Is there anything else you require?" Orb requested.

"No. Inform me the moment you have either of them," he stated.

Orb and He'lo studied each other before they nodded. Reynar ignored the gleam of greed in both of their eyes before they turned and exited the room. He returned his attention to Akita. She was standing at the window, looking out over the damaged cell block.

"Aren't you concerned they will find De'Mar before you do?" Reynar asked.

"I hope they do. Once he kills them, they will be out of my way," she answered with a shrug.

"What makes you think De'Mar can best them?" he asked, walking over and standing a short distance from her.

Her eyes flickered over the damage to his cheek again. "Because, brother, he already bested you," she stated, turning away.

Reynar narrowed his eyes as she walked across his office to the door. She didn't pause or look back. There had been something in her tone that bothered him. It sounded suspiciously like she was pleased that he had been bested.

Behr woke with a mild sense of disorientation. The slight rumble of the engines told him they were in motion again. A glance at the time showed he had slept over twelve hours. He froze when he felt a slight movement on the bed next to him.

He slid his hand over the cover. His fingers encountered a furry mass. Lifting his head, he noticed Pi curled up against his hip. He lowered his head and blinked when Chummy climbed up on his chest, circled around and laid back down with a wide yawn.

You sleep better than Raia. She snore and kick sometimes.

Behr remained still for a second, then reached up and touched the black and white spotted Quazin Chumloo. Chummy lifted his head and stared at him. He gently scratched the creature behind its ear.

"How do you communicate like this?" he asked.

All Chumloo can—if they bond with their pets, Chummy replied.

"Their pets? You think I am your pet?" he murmured.

Yes. You and Raia. You belong to Pi and me now, Chummy answered with a smug expression.

"Can you tell me about—Raia?" he asked.

Chummy wiggled his nose and looked at the door. Behr turned his head and followed the small creature's gaze. He gaped in astonishment when Chummy rose off the bed and floated over to the door.

I smell food!

Behr sat up. After glancing down at the bed, he noticed that Pi had already disappeared. He shook his head in wonder as Chummy floated out of his cabin. Pushing the covers aside, he rose from the bed and quickly dressed. He smiled when the tantalizing aroma of food caught his attention and his stomach growled.

"This has to be the strangest freighter crew I have ever encountered," he said, heading into the bathroom to finish freshening up.

∽

Several minutes later, he exited his cabin and walked across the corridor to the galley. Raia was humming under her breath as she prepared a meal. She glanced over her shoulder and smiled at him before returning her attention to the food she was preparing.

"Ander always loved cooking. He said the food tasted better than anything a replicator could prepare. He also said the art of cooking helps create a sense of calm and balance within our bodies. I'm still working on that part, but since the replicator died, I have to admit the homemade food is better," she said.

"I thought the only thing you had was cookies," he confessed from where he stood in the doorway, watching her.

Twin snorts from the table pulled his attention away from her, and he shrugged at the amused looks in Chummy and Pi's eyes. Raia had warned him that the two understood a lot more than most people thought they could.

"Is there anything I can do to help?" he asked.

She lifted her hand to her mouth. He watched the movement, captivated by the way she licked the droplet of sauce from the tip of her finger. His body reacted as much as his mind did. He had an unexpectedly intense urge to capture her finger with his tongue and suck on it.

He quickly looked up at her face when she cleared her throat. He didn't miss the rosy glow in her cheeks nor the way her gaze was locked on his lips, as if she imagined the same thing. The hiss of water boiling over the pot interrupted the moment, and she turned her back to him.

"You can set the table. There are plates and utensils in the third drawer down on the left," she said, waving to the cabinet next to the table.

He walked over, retrieved the items, and arranged four place settings. Pi and Chummy were seated in what looked like a child's seat that attached to the edge of the table. Unsure of what he should do, he retrieved two additional plates and placed one in front of each creature.

"Look out, this is hot," she warned.

He twisted around before stepping aside. She placed a large casserole dish on the table. He stood still, unsure of the protocol for the meal. She returned with two bottles of Curizan beer and a bowl of fruit.

"Is there anything else?" he asked.

She looked up from where she was dishing fruit onto the plates in front of Chummy and Pi. "Could you pour some Muza cream for these two? I'll have to make some more once we arrive at our destination," she said.

Behr nodded and completed the simple task, placing the two cups in front of the seemingly ravenous creatures devouring the fruit on their plates. The scene was so unexpected after the last month of his confinement that he chuckled and shook his head. Raia looked up at him with a questioning expression.

"I don't know if this is real or if I'm hallucinating," he confessed.

Raia laughed. "You're hallucinating, but we promise not to wake you up," she quipped.

He slid onto the seat across from her and filled his plate. "I don't feel like we've been properly introduced—or that I know what in the hell is going on," he admitted.

Her expression softened, and she paused, holding her fork in midair. She lowered it back to her plate. She fingered a chain around her neck and gripped something hidden under her shirt before releasing it with a deep sigh.

"My name is Raia Glossman. You already know that I'm human and that I was hired to break you out of prison. At the moment, it is too dangerous to meet up with your friends. I knew the Marastin Dow military establishment would be pissed off once they found out you had escaped, but I wasn't expecting them to send out their entire fleet. At the moment, my freighter looks like a Curizan research vessel since we are near one of the few sovereign sites the Marastin Dow have agreed not to attack. The Marastin Dow military ships are giving us some space, but it won't last long once we've passed through the safe zone. I've heard chatter on the underground communication links that Maradash has hired three of the best tracker assassins in the region to find us both—though of course he thinks I'm a Dregulon. Until we get out of Marastin Dow space, we need to keep a low profile. Once we are out, I'll notify your group to pick you up on Sanapare. It's located deep inside Curizan territory, so the Marastin Dow military aren't as likely to kill you there. Of course, the hired assassins will still be a problem, but it's the best I'm willing to do for a hundred thousand credits. If Maradash finds out I helped you, I'll have more than enough to worry about. The sooner we part ways, the safer it will be for me," she said.

Behr listened in silence. Raia pulled her gaze away and focused on her food. Regret filled him. His situation had placed her in danger. His thoughts turned to the rebellion that had begun before he was born.

"My father always believed that our people deserved more than a life filled with cruelty and death. He was a scientist—an archeologist. His primary focus was ancient civilizations. Normally, all Marastin Dow children are taken away from their parents when they are between five and seven years of age. They came for my older brother when I was three. When my mother resisted, they killed her and took him. My father returned three days later and found her nailed to the front door of our home," he said.

Raia stared at him in horror. "What happened to you?" she murmured.

"My father retrieved me from the spot where my mother had hidden me and took me away," he said.

"If he took you away, how did you end up back with the Marastin Dow military?" she asked.

"He and the others involved in the rebellion understood that in order for it to succeed, they would need people on the inside—those who knew the military and could hopefully recruit and lead," he explained.

She stared at him in disbelief. "Are you saying that your father and other parents sacrificed you and their kids to… to the cruelty and horrors they knew you would have to live through for their cause? Why didn't he just take you away? You could have gone to Ceran-Pax! There is a village there where anybody can live without fear, thanks to the Curizans. They are protected there," she said.

"We don't want to live on someone else's world, Raia. We want to live on our own world," he replied.

Raia looked down at her untouched food on her plate. He held back his groan of dismay. This was not a good conversation to share over a delicious meal.

"You mentioned that we needed to keep a low profile. Do you have a destination in mind?" he asked, changing the subject.

She looked up at him, the troubled look in her eyes fading, and nodded her head. "Yeah, it's a place along the rim between Marastin Dow and Sarafin space where Ander used to take me. We should be safe there," she said.

Behr relaxed and began to eat as Raia talked about some of the adventures Ander had taken her on. Several of them reminded him of those he had enjoyed with his father. He loved the way her eyes lit up as she laughed and the way her cheeks flushed. By the time the meal was over, all he could think about was how she must glow after an intense night of lovemaking.

CHAPTER SIX

Raia warily studied the Marastin Dow warship off her starboard bow. The warship was keeping pace with them. She checked the hologram disks. Everything was working correctly.

"Is there a problem?" Behr asked.

She glanced over her shoulder before checking her other sensors. "We've got a warship keeping pace with us. I don't like it," she replied.

He slid into the co-pilot seat. "That's a Destroyer. Even with the modifications that you've made to your freighter, you won't be able to outrun it," he observed in a grim voice.

"If they board us, they'll know this isn't a research ship," she added.

"We have another fifty clicks before they demand to board you. If they do…," he said.

"They won't," she interjected before turning in her seat. "Pi, I need you."

In seconds, Pi was sitting in front of her on the control dash. The Peek-aboo looked funny with the holographic image of the Destroyer projected on her small tan and white body. Pi gazed out the front windshield before turning back around and looking at her.

"Show me what you see," Raia quietly requested.

She lifted her hand and gently laid it against Pi's side. Closing her eyes, she waited for the images to come. A relieved smile curved her lips, and she opened her eyes again. Reaching out, she lifted Pi into her arms and snuggled with her for a moment before placing a kiss on Pi's small, furry head.

"I think that deserves some extra cookies. Don't forget to share them with Chummy," she murmured.

Pi clapped her tiny hands together and licked Raia's cheek before disappearing. Raia laughed and wiped the wet spot with her sleeve. She grinned at Behr's confused expression.

"We're going to be alright," she said with a confident expression.

"How do you know?" he asked.

"You'll see," she said.

Raia opened the communications system and locked on a rapidly closing warship. She hoped Pi's vision was right. If it was, they just might make it.

"Curizan *Challenger*, this is the Curizan research vessel CRV5126 requesting escort," she inquired.

"CRV5126, this is the Curizan Escort ship *Challenger*, acknowledging your request. Please stand by for further instructions," the communications tech stated.

∼

Captain K'lard Astar stood on the bridge of the Curizan Escort Ship *Challenger*, listening to the murmur of his crew's voices. On the screen in front of him, he could see an array of Marastin Dow warships spread out in an unusual formation. They appeared to be searching for something. The *Challenger* had encountered a Marastin Dow military blockade shortly after arriving through the jump gate. This was the second encounter with a large number of their ships.

"Sir, we've received a request from a Curizan research vessel for an escort," the communication tech announced.

K'lard noted the confused expression and the hesitancy in her voice. He walked over to her and looked at the research ship's signature. Everything appeared to be in order.

"What is the problem?" he asked.

"Sir, there is no way this can be the CRV5126," the tech replied.

"Why do you say that? The ship's signature and documentation appear to be in order," he said, studying the information on the screen.

"Yes, sir, on the screen it looks in order, but I'm sure that it isn't. My brother is on the CRV5126. I talked to him yesterday. He is working with the Valdier scientists on the Minor Moon of Leviathan," she said.

"Inform them we will provide an escort to the jump gate," a deep voice ordered.

K'lard straightened and lifted an eyebrow at the man standing a short distance behind him. He had been surprised when General Razdar Bahadur was transported over to his ship shortly before their last jump. He had heard stories of Bahadur, but this was the first time he had ever met the man. He returned his attention to the tech.

"Inform the ship to remain on their current path and that we will escort them as far as the jump gate," K'lard instructed.

"Yes, sir," the tech said, turning away.

K'lard stepped back and listened as the tech communicated his instructions. He called out an order to increase speed to intercept with the ship. Once he was finished, he looked at Bahadur and raised an eyebrow.

"You do realize if the Marastin Dow find out that we escorted a ship that wasn't one of ours, it will cause more than a few headaches for our diplomatic relations," he drawled.

Bahadur shrugged. "That is what the politicians are there for—to deal with the misunderstandings," he said.

K'lard shook his head as Bahadur turned and strode off the bridge. He returned his attention to the ship, wondering who would be crazy enough—other than Razdar Bahadur—to want to upset the entire Marastin Dow armada. He narrowed his gaze on the small dot moving in their direction.

"Ensign, get me intel on any recent activities in the region," he ordered.

"Yes, sir," the information ensign said.

"And tell my security chief I need to speak with him in my office," he instructed.

"Yes, sir. Captain off the bridge," the ensign replied as K'lard exited the room.

Several hours later, Raia breathed a sigh of relief when she saw the jump gate's lights ahead. There had been a few close calls involving a terse Marastin Dow captain insisting on boarding and searching their ship and the *Challenger's* captain threatening war if they did.

"CRV5126, this is the *Challenger*. The captain requested that you receive a current update of the surrounding regions. Unusual meteor activity has been detected that might damage your ship. Safe journeys and may your mission be successful," the tech said.

"CRV5126 acknowledges receipt of the incoming file. Safe journeys," Raia replied.

"It might be better to review what they've sent before I program the jump," she commented.

"I agree. I've never heard of meteor activity before in this area," Behr replied.

Raia tapped the file and pulled it to the side. It opened on the holograph screen between them. She frowned when a set of images appeared, and Behr loudly hissed in dismay.

"Well, they don't look like any meteors to me," she reflected with a skeptical expression.

"They are just as dangerous. The first one is a Triloug assassin named He'lo. He fought in the Triloug Civil War. He was court-martialed for killing three of his superior officers. He went underground and worked for whichever side would pay him the most. He kills for credits, but he also does it for pleasure. The second man is Orb. He is a Hoggian assassin from the Keltar regions. He started his life of crime at an early age—even by Marastin Dow standards. He slit the throats of his foster parents and escaped on a trade ship. He was caught and sent to prison where he learned how to hone his killing techniques. He led a prison riot on an Antrox mining prison. Eighty-three Antroxes and forty transport ship crew members were massacred. The prisoners escaped on the transports, and he was on one of them. We found the bodies of the escaped prisoners floating in space for a full click. He likes to work alone," he explained.

"They both sound wonderful... not. What about the woman?" she asked.

"Akita," he softly said.

She looked at him with a raised eyebrow. "The way you say her name, it makes me think you may have met her before," she said.

"I have. As you can tell, she is a Marastin Dow. She is far more dangerous than He'lo and Orb combined," he said.

Raia studied the woman. Her eyes were a strange reddish color with rings of white around them that matched her short white hair. Her face looked as if it were carved out of polished stone.

"She looks like a cyborg," she warily reflected.

Behr nodded. "She has been genetically enhanced. If Maradash enlisted these three, you might have rescued me for nothing," he said.

"If these three are as good as you say, then I think a change of plans may be in order," she said.

"What do you mean?" he asked.

She nodded at the screen. "They will be looking for you at the Spaceports and nearby planets. So, one way to throw them off is to go to a place where they would never think to look," she commented, programming in a new jump sequence.

"What if they do?" he asked.

"Then they better hope they can understand the language," she said with a grin.

"Where are we going?" Behr asked when they emerged from the jump gate.

He stared at the unfamiliar nebula spread out before them. Vivid colors of red, blue, green, and yellow illuminated what should have been deep space. A large red dwarf star, probably millions of light years away, cast an eerie glow, intermingling with the light cast by the small yellow stars. A field of asteroids, varying from hundreds to millions of miles apart, created a series of rings between them and the nebula.

"To my hidden fortress," she said with a smile.

"You have a hidden fortress?" he asked.

She grinned and nodded. "Yep."

"Do you mind if I ask where we are exactly?" he prodded.

"The area is called the Triangulum. It is well off the main transport lanes, so nobody uses this jump gate," she replied.

"Why?" he asked.

She nodded. "Because of this," she quietly responded.

Behr frowned when he saw a hazy purple cloud spread out before them. The translucent appearance was deceiving. As the cloud engulfed them, visibility dropped to near zero.

"Switching to manual override," she said.

"Is that a...?" his voice faded.

Raia had pulled up a map and was guiding them through a minefield of dead ships after switching on a series of low-level lights to illuminate their way. Behr read the name of a ship as they passed —*Mercy*.

The Mercy was lost nearly two hundred and fifty years ago, he thought.

The *Mercy* was a Marastin Dow tanker ship. There were twenty-five crew members and three officers aboard at the time of its disappearance. The records speculated that it perished during the Great War between the Sarafin, Valdier, and Curizans.

"This whole area is littered with spaceships. Do you see the asteroids with the purple light?" she asked.

Behr's gaze moved to one of the asteroids with a faint glimmer that reminded him of the color of lavender. The asteroid almost appeared to be wrapping itself around the ship. A shiver of unease slid through him.

"Take a look at how the rock appears to be growing around the ship. Ander said it is some type of parasite that lives within the asteroids and exists only in this cloud. If you look at the readings, there is a larger composition of nitrogen, with a hint of methane. They feed on the methane, but they love oxygen. When a ship comes too close, they attach to it and eat through the outer hull, sucking all the oxygen out," she explained.

He shook his head in wonder. "How did Ander discover this?" he asked.

"According to him, he met a short-range freighter captain. The man was the sole survivor out of a crew of ten. This captain told him about this place off the normal trading route. He said he'd purchased a stone tablet that described an abandoned planet held within a mystical ring that was filled with riches, and he babbled about this living rock that devoured ships. Ander thought the man was crazy until he pulled out the tablet. It was old… really, really, really old. Anyway, Ander convinced the man to draw a map, write everything he had seen, and describe in detail how he managed to escape. Ander also persuaded the captain to sell him the tablet. Although from what Ander told me, it didn't take much to persuade the man. I guess the captain felt the tablet was cursed," she explained.

Fascinated, he stared at the ship graveyard stretched out in front of them. "What did Ander do?" he asked.

"He found a mythical planet," she replied with a grin. "The tablet was written in an ancient language, but what was even more fascinating was that there was a hollowed-out section in the stone that contained a map showing safe passage through the asteroid field."

Behr's eyes widened when the *EA II* broke through the cosmic cloud. In the distance, a bright blue and white planet shimmered against the backdrop of a brilliant yellow sun. He leaned forward, staring at the planet in awe.

"Does the planet have a name?" he asked.

Raia laughed. "Yes, but Ander renamed it. Welcome to Planet Raia," she said with a soft smile.

CHAPTER SEVEN

Raia increased power to the front shield as they began their entry into the planet's atmosphere. Pride welled in her when they broke through the clouds, and she heard Behr's hiss of astonishment. Planet Raia's beauty easily competed with the lush landscape and deep oceans found on the Valdier, Sarafin, and Curizan home worlds.

They flew over a brilliant blue ocean. As they neared the coast, the water became so clear that the vivid, colorful patterns on the coral were visible in the depths. A dark, swirling mass showed a thriving marine life below the waves. Birds flew off the cliffs as Raia began their descent.

A waterfall at least a thousand feet high spilled over and poured into the ocean along the cliff wall. Tall pillars stood on each side of the falls. The weathered remains of twin mystical warriors, whose spears formed an arch over the waterfall, guarded an enchanting city made of stone and glass.

Behr stared down at the city with a combination of awe and confusion. How could something so beautiful be deserted? Where were the inhabitants?

Graceful six-legged gazelle-like creatures, startled by the freighter's approach, leaped away. Raia set the ship down in the center of an empty plaza and shut off the engines. They sat in silence for several minutes, staring out of the windshield.

Raia laughed when Chummy and Pi ran onto the bridge and began excitedly jumping around with joy. She rose from her seat. Her changing expressions communicated that she must be conversing with the two.

"What are they saying?" he curiously asked, rising from his seat.

She laughed again. "That I'm taking way too long. They love it here," she said.

"I can understand why. What I don't understand is why there are no inhabitants," he wondered.

She smiled at him and waved. "Come on. I'll show you," she said, holding out her hand.

Her excitement was contagious. He gripped her outstretched hand and let her pull him along. Chummy floated down the corridor. The small Chumloo made him laugh when his little legs moved as if he were running while his long fluffy tail flowed like a dragon's tail.

Pi was popping in and out. Sometimes she was ahead of them, and other times she was behind them, impatiently pushing them along. He was amazed when both creatures swept by the galley without stopping.

Raia must have seen his surprised expression, because she said, "Trust me, the fruit here is far superior to anything we could find at a Spaceport market. The only place that has fruit this good is on Ceran-Pax. Ben and Aaron are experts when it comes to cultivating fresh fruits and vegetables."

She released his hand and strode across the holding bay to press the button that lowered the platform. Chummy and Pi disappeared the moment the door was opened far enough for them to squeeze through the gap. Raia was practically dancing with suppressed energy as she waited for the platform to lower all the way.

A knot formed in Behr's throat as he watched her. Over the past several days, emotions that he didn't realize he possessed had flared to life. The more time he spent with Raia and her two adorable pets, the more he wanted.

He followed Raia at a slower pace as she hurried down the ramp. Despite the beauty and grandeur of the city, it was nothing compared to Raia. Her hair flowed around her like the wind-driven waves of the ocean. Her laughter echoed through the plaza.

It was impossible to miss the way her dark blue shirt hugged her full breasts and her black trousers clung to her hips. She twisted around and waved for him to follow her. In that instant, an intense emotion hit him hard.

I'm falling in love with her, he realized.

He reached out, gripped one of the platform's support rods, and stared at her. He rebelled against the idea while his heart hammered against his chest. The happy expression on her face faded to one of uncertainty. She slowly walked back up the platform until she was standing in front of him.

"It's okay. There isn't anything here that will hurt you," she reassured him.

He looked down at her and shook his head. "It isn't that," he confessed in a voice that sounded deeper than normal.

"What is it then?" she asked.

The wide-eyed innocence staring back at him in concern was his undoing. He groaned, reached out, and caressed her cheek. How could someone tough enough to break into a Marastin Dow prison and free him be so refreshingly innocent at the same time?

A curious smile curved her lips. Before he could decipher its meaning, she stepped forward and pressed her lips against his. A jolt of surprise struck him before it was quickly followed by pure pleasure.

He wrapped his arms around her and pulled her against him. Passion built into a powerful physical need, and for a moment, he was almost afraid he would crush her. She slid her hands up his arms, leaving a burning path on his skin under his light-weight, long-sleeved shirt.

The fire spread when her fingertips grazed the heated flesh on his neck before she threaded them through his short black hair. His groan of need rumbled in his chest as he slid his hand down and cupped her buttocks, pressing her firmly against his engorged cock. He captured her soft whimper as he deepened their kiss.

Visions of fireworks exploded through his mind when she partially lifted her leg and the slight change in position was enough to nestle his throbbing cock against her womanhood. He pulled back, ending the kiss.

The expression on her face was just as he'd imagined. Her eyes were closed, her cheeks rosy, and her lips swollen and moist. Her head remained tilted back, so he leisurely placed several short, passionate kisses along her jaw and down the column of her slender throat.

"So, this is what I've been missing out on," she breathed.

Her barely audible words caused him to stiffen in surprise. He silently repeated what she had said before slowly straightening. He must have been mistaken. There was no way she could have responded so passionately if she had never—

"Raia… would you be offended if I asked how many men you have kissed before?" he asked.

She opened her eyes and looked up at him. Her eyes glimmered with a combination of amusement and a residual unfocused look caused by their passion. He dropped his when she stepped back and gave him a cheeky grin.

"No, I won't be offended. Come on, I want to show you something before it gets dark, and it will take us a while to get there," she said.

He didn't miss the way she left his question unanswered. Sighing deeply, he shook his head and ruefully ran a hand over his still engorged cock. He hoped they were walking because he suspected it would take a while for his libido to cool off. It had been a long, long time since he experienced this kind of situation.

"What about the freighter?" he asked, following her down the platform.

"It will be fine. We're the only ones on the planet who can fly it. Besides, Chummy and Pi will be back soon. They love hiding their new treasures onboard and going out for more," she said.

"How do you know we are the only ones on the planet?" he asked.

She shrugged. "Because in the over twenty years of coming here, neither Ander nor I ever saw anyone. This place has been my home base for the past ten years. I think if there had been anyone else, I would have seen them by now," she replied.

He raised his eyebrow and nodded. It seemed inconceivable that she hadn't encountered someone over such a long period. He closed the distance between them as they walked across the plaza.

"Did you ever discover who lived here?" he asked.

She shrugged and waved to the two statues poised on each side of the waterfall. "Ander deduced that there had been many different kinds of species coexisting here at one time. Ander thought the debris field is the remainder of an asteroid belt that was comprised of the destroyed planets in this star system, gravitationally locked by the sun. There also appears to have been another sun, far enough away not to destroy this planet when it imploded, but it did destroy life on a few others. I remember seeing images of the ruins during one of Ander's scouting trips. Anyway, Ander speculated that between the devastation of the other worlds and the danger of trying to pass through the asteroid belt, the inhabitants simply left. I know Ander had to do a lot of repairs to the jump gate after we arrived. It's a really old model, and even though we came through with no issues, he didn't trust it enough to take us back out safely. Ander was saying a few choice words about that. He never was a big fan of space walking, since getting into the suits was a pain in the ass because of his tail," she sadly reminisced.

"I would like to explore the city more while we are here," he said.

"That won't be a problem. I just happen to have the vehicles we'll need to do that," she stated.

They stepped through a large covered entrance to a domed building. A large, dusty tarp, tied down along the edges, was draped over what he suspected was one of the vehicles Raia had mentioned. He helped release the straps and remove the cover. He was fascinated by the vehicle revealed underneath.

"I've never seen anything like this," he confessed.

He slowly walked around the slick silver transport. Through the clear front windshield, he could see black bucket seats with additional seating behind. Winged doors on either side allowed access to the interior. As he walked around the transport's rear end, he noticed twin turbines.

Raia opened one of the doors, reached in, and pressed a button. He stared in wonder as the clear fuselage came alive in front of him. A steady stream of glowing dark purple liquid flowed through thin tubes and circulated around a chamber of pale lavender gas. In the center of the chamber was an intense blue flame.

"These look suspiciously like the parasites we saw on the debris field," he commented, looking up at her over the fuselage.

"They are. Don't ask me how they got in there or who was crazy enough to use them. Whoever did it was super creative, and the engineering is incredible. This thing has phenomenal power, and as far as I can tell, the energy hasn't depleted at all since we first found this place. Ander suspected the parasites are in some type of hibernation while they are in the gas. They die off at a much slower rate. When the engine is in use, oxygen is introduced with the methane. What we did learn is that if you pump too much oxygen into the tank, the parasites die pretty quickly," she said.

"That would be a good thing if one of the cylinders were damaged and they escaped. Otherwise, I could see them devouring the entire planet," he replied with a look of distaste.

"Yeah. I guess they are like us. They need that sweet spot to live," she mused.

"Would you mind if I piloted this thing—now that I don't have to worry about destroying your world," he teased.

She laughed. "Well, as long as you swear not to ruin my planet, I guess so," she responded with an exaggerated sigh.

The teasing in her voice and her playful expression reawakened his barely calmed desire. He rounded the vehicle until he stood in front of her. She reached up, grabbed his shirt with both hands, and tilted her head back.

"What is it about you that makes me want to...," he muttered before he shook his head.

"It's my charming personality and because I want you to shut up and kiss me again," she said, sliding her arms around his neck. "You know, for an uptight military man, I find you rather fascinating," she whispered a breath away from his lips.

Raia didn't know what was wrong with her. She had never been so brazen in her life—well, not when it came to a desire to crawl all over a guy. Evetta had said there might be explosions in her brain when she kissed the right guy, and she was right. From Behr's reaction to their first kiss, she really hoped it was a sign that he had felt the same thing. One thing was for sure, his body wasn't immune to their physical contact!

She pressed her parted lips on his, savoring the intense response swelling inside her. Her nipples hardened and an unfamiliar tightness was increasing between her legs.

She did know about the physical side of a relationship. In her years as a freighter captain, she had found out a few things. Hell, being around Ben, Evetta, Hanine, and Aaron for ten months was enough of an education on the physical intimacy between a man and woman! It was just that the physical aspect had never happened to her personally outside some vidcoms she watched and a little self-experimentation, of course.

No, this is way better, she silently thought as she tangled her tongue with his.

Behr leaned into her, pressing her back against the transport. She tugged at his shirt, pulling the back free from his trousers. She slid her hands along his bare skin, her fingers skimming over the smooth flesh of his lower back until she came across a scar and then another… and another. The vivid realization of what the marks were pierced the heated passion engulfing her mind and body, and a wave of cold reality hit her.

Raia tilted her head back, breaking the kiss while she unconsciously caressed one of the long scars. The image of another man's back covered in deep scars rose in her mind.

"What happened to you?" she softly inquired.

CHAPTER EIGHT

*B*ehr pulled away from Raia, ignoring his feeling of disappointment at the intrusion of reality into their moment of intimacy. He stepped away and tucked his shirt back into his trousers. Over the years, he had forgotten about the scars on his back. Some of the women he had been with never mentioned it, while others thought that it was part of his heritage as a Marastin Dow warrior.

"I'll tell you along the way," he said.

The conflicting emotions that crossed her face made him smile. He closed the distance between them and kissed her hard on the lips. Caressing her cheek, he soothed the frown line near her mouth.

"Don't leave out any details," she softly ordered.

He started in surprise when she turned her head and nipped his thumb before ducking under his arm and sliding into the transport. He chuckled under his breath and shook his head. Once again, she had knocked him off-balance.

Once Behr slid into the pilot's seat, the transport's doors closed around them. He studied the panel before him with a feeling of déjà vu. The system setup was very similar to the modern designs.

"How long ago did Ander think the last inhabitants were here?" he asked.

"I'm not sure, a few centuries at the most. We found three vehicles in a sealed storage unit under this building. At first, we wondered if someone landed here and left them, but after seeing the fuselage, Ander decided they were probably abandoned by the original inhabitants. I received my first piloting lessons with them," she added.

He flexed his fingers and gripped the control wheel. "You said this thing has some power?" he inquired.

"Oh yeah," she said, pulling on her restraint straps.

He pressed the power button beside the control wheel. When he pulled back on the wheel, the transport rose off the ground a short distance and floated forward. Raia raised an eyebrow and gave him an unimpressed look. He grinned and applied more pressure.

The force of the acceleration pushed both of them back against their seats. Raia uttered a delighted squeal as they shot out over the city's twin guardians. He angled the transport down the cliff face.

Raia gripped the armrest and pressed her feet against the floorboard. He quickly pulled the transport's nose up ten feet from the surface. Water from a wave splashed onto the windshield and the automated wiper blades turned on.

"I did the same thing two weeks after Ander said I had graduated from my training," she said with a breathless laugh.

"What did Ander do?" he asked.

She relaxed in her seat. "He grounded me and made me retake his entire course all over again," she replied. "Goddess, but I miss him."

He frowned at the note of longing and sadness in her voice. "What happened to him?"

"Two Marastin Dow warships attacked us on my birthday. Ander held them off so I could escape. We were supposed to meet up on Ceran-

Pax, but he never showed up. I know they killed him. I just never understood why," she murmured.

He noticed that she grabbed the chain she wore around her neck. Through the gap in her shirt, he glimpsed a pendant. Reaching out, he cupped her free hand.

"How old were you?" he asked.

She looked at him. Tears made her eyes appear to shimmer in the afternoon sunlight coming through the windows. She cast him a quavering smile.

"Fourteen. It was the same day I found Chummy and Pi. I don't know what I would have done without them," she confessed.

"But… you said you know Ben, Aaron, and the two Marquette sisters. Surely, they were there for you," he said.

She nodded. "They were. At least they were as much as I let them," she amended with a rueful expression. "I was fourteen and thought I knew everything."

"You were too young to be traveling alone," he muttered.

"I wasn't alone. I had Chummy and Pi and one hell of a decked-out freighter thanks to Evetta and Hanine. I did alright. I had enough credits to get by until I received my first job. Pi and Chummy helped keep me safe," she added.

"I'm still trying to figure those two out," he confessed.

"Chummy can read the minds of those around us. He can also absorb information through touch. You already know about his ability to levitate. Pi, on the other hand, is a master of getting in and out of places and spying on the unwary. She can telekinetically manipulate some things, like locks, doors, and windows. Her strongest gift is precognition. She can only see about twenty-four-to-forty-eight hours ahead into the future, but it is usually plenty of time to plan for things," she explained.

"She can see the future? Can she do it for everything?" he asked.

Raia shook her head. "No. Her visions are the clearest when there is danger involved, especially if it is going to happen when she is around. I think that is how her species continues to survive. She usually knows when and where to be for an upcoming job, but not always who it will be for," she said.

"Has she ever been wrong?" he curiously inquired.

Raia was quiet for a moment before she nodded. "Once. She thought Ander was alive and that if we went to a particular spot, he would be there," she murmured.

"Where was that?" he asked.

She leaned her head back against the seat and stared out of the windshield. "Planet Raia," she softly answered.

The sadness in Raia's voice swept over Behr. He wished he had the power to take it away. He reached over and cupped her hand.

"You asked about my scars. Marastin youths are indoctrinated at a very young age in the ways of war. We are trained to be brutal, uncaring, and to succeed using any method," he explained.

"You were whipped?" she inquired, squeezing his hand.

"Yes… many times," he said with a wry grin. "I had an issue with authority. It took a while for me to realize while those training us wanted us to turn on each other, they did not appreciate it when one of us turned on them."

Raia shook her head. "How can people be so cruel against each other? I don't think I'll ever understand it. Ander could be scary when he needed to be, but he was also very gentle and caring. He would never harm someone else for the fun of it," she said.

"Most Marastin Dow don't want to hurt others, Raia. They are trained at a young age to be that way," he quietly replied.

"Well, that is just wrong," she stated.

He chuckled. "Yes, it is. That's why we are doing something about it," he said.

Two hours later, Behr landed the transport along the bank of a river bordered by a dense jungle. When Raia had instructed him to turn inland, he was skeptical about their destination. They spent most of their time flying over a sea of green canopy. He was surprised when he saw the landing pad. He would have missed it if Raia hadn't pointed it out.

"This is incredible. How did you ever find it?" he asked, powering down the transport.

"Ander always had an eye for anything that was out of the ordinary. I guess I learned it from him. I found this place the last time I was here," she said.

The doors opened, and they exited the vehicle. Raia reached into the back seat, grabbed a weapon, and walked around the transport to a path that led into the jungle.

"Are you sure there is nothing here that is dangerous?" he warily asked.

"Well, there might be a few scary things. If it helps, you can carry this... just in case," she said.

He took the weapon she held out. "And... when were you going to tell me that this might be needed?" he dryly inquired.

She laughed and ran the tips of her fingers across his chest. "Right after you told me how you got the scars on your back. Don't think I've forgotten," she said, walking past him.

He remained where he was for a moment, gazing at her as she started walking down the covered path. Shaking his head, he followed her. He stepped closer to her as they came to a fork in the dimly lit path, and she took the darker trail leading deeper into the jungle. Low-level lighting illuminated the stone path as they neared and faded shortly after they passed.

"This technology rivals that of today," he commented.

"At times it is more advanced," she said.

"You said you found this place the last time you came to the planet?" he asked.

Raia nodded. "Yes. It looks like some kind of temple. The jungle has covered most of it," she explained.

Rays of sunlight pierced sections of the canopy, casting eerie halos of light all around them. The climate was humid but not unbearable. As they wound their way deeper into the jungle, they traversed several stone bridges spanning the crystal clear streams.

"How did you ever find this?" he wondered out loud.

She laughed. "You'd never believe me," she replied.

"Why not?" he asked.

She paused and stared in silence at the path in front of them. "Because I'm not even sure it was real," she murmured.

He stepped up behind her and looked over her head. The path disappeared around the bend ahead of them. A surreal feeling swept through him. It felt as if he were standing on the edge of a magical discovery.

"What was it?" he pressed, needing to know.

She unconsciously leaned back against him. "I had finished a successful but dangerous run and needed a place to go for a few weeks until things calmed down. My birthday was coming up, and I always spend it here. It's the one place where I feel closer to Ander. I was exploring the area in the transport when I saw the landing pad. Once I landed, I noticed the path and followed it," she said.

He slowly turned her around until she was facing him. He noticed that she avoided looking into his eyes. Lifting his hand, he gently tilted her chin up until she was looking at him.

"There is more to your story," he suspected.

She pulled her chin out of his hand and uttered a strained laugh. "Isn't there always?" she quipped, trying to turn away from him.

"What did you see, Raia?" he quietly asked.

She lowered her head. "Ghosts," she mumbled.

He frowned and remained where he was as she twisted away and continued down the path. Surely, he must have misunderstood what she said. He quickly caught up to her.

"What kind of ghosts?" he asked, warily scanning the area.

She laughed and shook her head. "I don't know. Are there different kinds? It was gold, it floated, it led me to the place we are going to now, and then it disappeared. So, I guess you could call it a Golden Ghost. Goldie for short," she chuckled and shook her head again. "It was a crazy day. The Tiliqua I rescued had a nasty cold and gave it to me. I was probably hallucinating. What is cool, though, is that I didn't hallucinate this," she declared with a wave of her hand.

Behr followed her hand motion and gasped. Standing before them was a beautiful domed building. Lush vines, covered in a variety of flowers, clung to the curved walls. Exotic birds, some half the size of the transport, roosted in a tree that rose nearly a hundred feet into the air. Thick branches had grown down from the outstretched limbs and buried themselves in the rich, moist soil, giving the tree extra stability.

"That's a Baba tree. The Sola birds love the fruit it produces," she explained.

"Sola birds?" he repeated, staring in wonder at the vibrant blue, red, orange, green, and yellow-feathered birds.

"If you listen when they sing, it's like they are saying so-la, so-la," she said, singing the last part.

Behr listened as the birds imitated Raia. Their song wasn't loud or harsh but soft and melodic. A few birds started the song but more joined in the chorus, and their music pulsed as if it was the jungle's heartbeat.

"This is incredible," he confessed.

"There's more," she quietly said, grasping his hand and lightly tugging on it.

He allowed her to pull him along. As they rounded the structure, he saw a thirty-foot-long arched roof held up by a series of round pillars protecting the dome's entrance. The diversity of plants, animals, and insects awoke the scientist deep inside him. He couldn't help but admire the flowering vines spiraling around each pillar. Tiny rodents scurried for cover, and a wide variety of insects fluttered from one flower to another.

I could spend a lifetime studying the flora alone, he thought.

Another pang of regret struck him when he thought of his father and how much he would have loved being here. This was one of the worlds his father had lived to discover. From the bits and pieces that Raia had shared about Ander, he suspected that the man had felt the same way. He could appreciate Ander's intense fascination with the planet.

They entered the dome. He noted the interior was composed of rows of partially sheltered stadium-like seating. Behr walked around Raia and slowly explored the upper perimeter. He carefully studied the interior, noting the center platform at the bottom.

Over time, the foliage from the jungle had crept inside. Vines covered most of the low interior walls. The ceiling of the dome remained intact, though more vines fought to cover the immense pillars supporting the dome and portions of the floor.

"When I first saw this place, it made me think of the amphitheaters where Ander took me to see live performances. I can almost see a troupe of players decked out in fanciful costume. The only thing I can't understand is why anyone would build something like this so far away from the city," she said.

Behr paused by one of the pillars to study a carved figure frozen in time. It was clearly a Tiliqua from the short stature and double heads. The Tiliqua was holding a large tablet, representative of their species' business acumen. He continued around the upper level, pausing and studying each figure featured inside an alcove.

Stunned disbelief struck him when he reached the all-too-familiar pose of a male and female Marastin Dow. The woman was casually dressed in a pair of trousers and a mid-thigh tunic. He lifted his hand and ran his fingers over the digital scanner that she was holding. The man was pointing upward. Behr followed the direction of the statue's hand. His breath caught in his throat at the realization of where they were at.

"This was not a theater for the arts, but one of science and learning. This was a place where some of the greatest minds in the galaxy once gathered," he called out, staring up at a map of the stars.

Raia turned from where she stood in the center of the amphitheater and looked up the ceiling. Now that he mentioned it, she took her time observing the different statues. There was a statue for almost every known species in the galaxy.

What she didn't understand was if so many different species had lived here, why did they abandon this section of the star system? The city had been devoid of any diversity. Ander searched high and low for evidence of who had lived here. The only statues in the city were the two warriors on each side of the waterfall.

She climbed the steps until she was standing on the platform. Patterns on the floor reminded her of star charts. She twisted and turned, as if dancing to silent music, as she tried to identify each star system.

"The Valdier, the Sarafin, the Curizan, and… this one. I don't recognize the others," she murmured.

She stepped toward the center of the platform, following a deep line carved into the thick stone. A tingling sensation against her skin made her touch the pendant hanging from her neck. Surprise engulfed her when she noticed it was pulsing.

Lifting the pendant from the valley between her breasts, she started in surprise when it pulled away from her hand and floated in the air. It was pulling her toward the center of the platform. She resisted the urge to follow the tug.

"Behr, my pendant is doing something really strange!" she called.

Out of the corner of her eye, she saw him hurry down the steps. He stepped close and examined the pulsing crystal hovering in the air. Raia pulled the chain over her head, keeping a firm grip on the metal rope when it drew taut.

"Let go of it," he said.

The chain rubbed against the skin of her fingers before she released it. She slowly followed the pendant as it floated through the air. It reminded her of a ship caught in a tractor beam.

Or Chummy on an average day getting into the cookie cabinet, she silently mused.

The moment the pendant reached the center of the platform, a thin laser beam of light burst from it. She blinked and looked down. Behr stepped close to her, pulling her aside when red lights fanned out along the thin lines carved into the stone. They stumbled back when a pillar rose from the center and the holographic form of a woman appeared.

"Welcome home, explorers. If you are receiving this message, then our people have survived. There is much to explain," the woman said with a serene smile.

Raia reached for Behr when he pulled away from her and stepped forward. His eyes were glued to the woman. A vein along his temple throbbed, and his throat moved as if he were trying to say something. Concerned, Raia reached for him.

"What is it?" she asked.

"Look at her," he murmured, his eyes focused on the woman standing on the platform.

Raia looked at the woman with a frown. It took a moment for her to understand why he was so shocked. She kept looking from him to the hologram and back again.

"She's a Marastin Dow," she finally said.

He nodded. "She is much more than that. She is… was… my mother," he announced.

CHAPTER NINE

*R*aia ran her fingers through her damp hair as she exited the bathroom in her cabin. Her mind whirled with everything they had learned today—and her heart hurt for Behr. They had listened to the woman's introduction a half dozen times. Before leaving, they searched the building and found a hidden compartment embedded in the column at the base of the hologram projector. Inside was a computer crystal containing more information.

Neither one of them had said much on the way back to the freighter. She had piloted them, while Behr sat in silence, fingering the disk. She had prepared a light dinner, which he barely touched before he disappeared into his cabin.

Behr hurting? Chummy asked, peering up at her from her bed.

"Yes… he is hurting," she murmured.

You make better? Chummy asked.

Raia smiled. "He'll be alright. He just needs a little time," she said.

Snuggles help, Chummy suggested.

Laughing, Raia affectionately scratched Chummy behind the ear. "Yes, snuggles do help. It looks like you and Pi found quite the assortment of treasures today," she teased.

Chummy rubbed his rounded belly and fell over onto his side. Pi was sprawled out in the center of her bed snoring. The Peekaboo was surrounded by fruit, nuts, and an assortment of odd trinkets that she had found fascinating.

"You know, you two really need to keep your treasures in your own beds, not mine. It will take me an hour to clear everything off," she gently admonished.

Chummy smacked his lips and pulled himself over until he was curled up next to Pi. Raia knew it was a pointless argument. They did this every time they journeyed anywhere. Her bed always seemed to be their go-to place when they got back from their exploring.

Sighing, she shook her head and decided she would grab a hot beverage and check the scanners. Despite never meeting anyone here, old habits die hard. The last thing she wanted was to become complacent.

She exited her cabin and walked the short distance down the corridor. The sound of a woman's voice drew her to Behr's cabin. The door was open, and she paused at the entrance.

"Post supernova: Year Four hundred twenty-five: This documentary is provided for any returning survivors in the hope that it will help them understand what has happened here in the event that none of those who remained behind survive.

"Several generations ago, scientists predicted the star we called Nebulona was on the verge of going supernova. The inhabitants of the closest planets began evacuating to the Marastin Dow home world. The star's instability increased more quickly than expected. Fear spread that the binary star gravitationally locked with it would also explode, destroying all life in this star system. The decision was made that an exploratory mission was necessary. A group of our highest-ranking officers were dispatched to find a suitable planet for the inhabitants of our world. There was hope that we could settle on the Valdier,

Sarafin, or Curizan worlds, but the commanders believed we would not be accepted. We wouldn't know until they returned."

"How far have you watched?" she quietly asked.

Behr looked up from where he was sitting on his bed. "Just the first part," he responded.

She walked over, sat down on the bed, and scooted up until she was sitting next to him. He placed a pillow behind her back. The simple, thoughtful gesture sent a wave of warmth through her.

"Thank you," she murmured.

"I had to modify the vidcom reader to get it to work," he said.

Raia looked at the portable vidcom displayer. Behr had removed the outer casing and adjusted the drive bay to hold the crystal in place so the laser could read the information.

"You're pretty creative when you need to be," she teased.

He chuckled. "It has come in handy at times," he admitted.

"I guess we should find out what happened next," she said.

He nodded and pressed the play button. The frozen image flickered. She unconsciously reached down and grasped Behr's hand when the woman began to speak again.

"The description of the final events of our civilization is based on written and verbal documentation left by those that survived the initial blasts that hit the planet. Post Supernova: Year One: The first waves of destruction from the supernova destroyed the home worlds of the Tiliqua, the Gelatians, the Antrox, and the Dregulons. The ripple effect from the first shockwaves caused severe damage to our planet. Tsunamis, earthquakes, intense weather patterns, and volcanic eruptions were reported worldwide, with ninety percent of the cities destroyed. There was a prediction of stronger shockwaves and tidal waves to follow. With the fear of a second explosion, the Council of Scientists decided that an immediate evacuation of the planet was necessary. Only a few key scientists would remain.

"No one really understood the amount of devastation that was to follow. Reports began coming in of a large asteroid field between our planet and deep space. Four thousand and six ships out of five thousand were lost. The asteroids were remnants of the destroyed planets and were said to contain a magnetic property that pulled the ships toward them. Reports intercepted during the mass evacuation relayed there was a living parasite inside the asteroids that engulfed the ships, entrapping them. Attempts to rescue the passengers ended with the rescuers becoming entrapped. No one was spared."

"Ander reversed the magnetic field on the outer hull. I did the same to the *EA II*. That is how we were able to get through," she murmured.

"A negative against a negative or positive against a positive, thus repelling each other," he murmured.

"A decision was made today for the evacuation of those remaining on the planet. Our engineers have made a break-through on engine technology, and we believe that we can safely navigate through the asteroid belt. A rudimentary jump gate has been constructed and will be deployed once we make it off the planet.

"I'm hesitant to leave, but there are so few of us left. Any hope that others will one day return have faded. I'll admit that I'm scared. My fear is that no one survived, which is why they never returned. Most of my peers believe that the survivors concluded this planet is no longer viable—or perhaps doesn't even exist any longer." The woman looked down at her hands and was silent for a moment before she looked up again. *"My expertise is in horticulture. I understand how plants survive—and know how difficult it will be to keep them alive in space. If we do find others of our kind still alive, I hope that once they know our home world is still habitable, they... I can return. If you are watching this, then my dream has come true, and I would like to be the first to welcome you home."*

The holographic image flickered before fading out. Raia's heart twisted with grief when Behr took a long, shuddering breath. She squeezed his hand in sympathy.

"There have always been rumors of a forgotten world. I was young, but I remember some details and I do have fragmented memories of my mother. She loved digging in the soil. I remember that she used to carry me on her back as she walked along rows of vegetables she had cultivated. She wasn't like the other women. She was gentle and kind. My father seldom talked about her. I remember asking him once why she was different. He said that she came from another world—a world far different from the one that the Marastin Dow lived in now. He was searching for that world when he was captured by Maradash," he murmured.

Raia twisted around until she was facing him. She lifted a hand and smoothed back a tuft of his hair that had fallen forward over his forehead. It was still slightly damp from his shower.

"I found the crystal disk in the spine of a book Ander gave me on the day the Marastin Dow attacked us. He had gone to an antique dealer's shop on Sanapare. Do you think it is possible that your father gave the disk to Ander to keep it safe from Maradash?"

"He must have. They were a lot alike. I don't remember my father ever talking about Ander; but then, he seldom mentioned names to me for fear that they would be intercepted by my superiors," he admitted.

"Do you know what happened to your father?" she asked.

"He was executed fourteen years ago," he said.

Compassion filled Raia. "I'm sorry," she said.

Behr caressed her cheek. "You are an extraordinary woman, Raia Glossman," he murmured.

Raia leaned into him when he slid his arm around her. She slipped her leg over his until she was straddling his lap. Desire filled her, and she knew that tonight she wouldn't have to worry about cleaning off her bed—at least she hoped she wouldn't.

"I want to stay with you tonight," she whispered.

Her eyelashes lowered when he leaned forward and kissed her. She slid her arms around his neck and parted her lips. This kiss was different from the earlier ones. There were the usual fireworks going off inside her, but there was also something else—a hint of vulnerability to open herself to him in a way that she had never done to anyone before.

She caught her breath when he slid his hands under her oversized shirt, and cupped her breasts. She sucked hard on his tongue when he pinched her taut nipples. Her hips seemed to have a mind of their own, and she began rubbing against his engorged cock.

Time slowed down as he released her lips. Their eyes remained locked as he gripped her shirt and lifted it over her head. Raising her arms caused her breasts to thrust forward. Shock and desire made a scorching path through her when he leaned in and captured one of her nipples between his lips.

"Holy cosmos!" she exclaimed as heat flooded her nether regions.

She curled her fingers in his hair to keep him from releasing her. Intense waves of desire swept through her, and she began to rock while tiny moans of passion slipped from her lips. He continued to torture her nipple with a combination of deep sucks and flicks of his tongue.

His fingers were busy at the same time. Her pajama pants and panties were no match against his explorations. He pushed both pieces of fabric down as far as they would go and caressed her buttocks. Her breathing turned from soft gasps to hiccups.

"I want to explore you," he muttered against her breasts.

"I think I'm going to self-combust," she warned him.

His soft chuckle brushed across her sensitive flesh, and she feared her prediction was about to come true. He twisted, pushing her down onto the bed. Now, he was the one straddling her.

Raia groaned in protest when he lifted her arms and began pushing them away from his shoulders. Sliding his hands along her arms to her wrists, he slowly lifted them until they were over her head while lavishing pleasure on her straining nipples.

"Keep them there," he instructed.

"But… but… I want to touch you," she complained.

The heated breath of his laugh caressed her bare stomach this time. She rocked her hips, straining to get closer. He was driving her crazy!

"If you touch me, Raia, things will be over faster than I want them to be," he cautioned.

She smiled in pleasure at the strained note in his voice. She closed her eyes, thankful to know she wasn't the only one losing control. Curiosity and excitement built inside her at the thought.

She lifted her hips when he tugged on her pajama bottoms. The cool air brushing her heated skin was quickly replaced by warm lips against her inner thigh. She popped her eyes open and caught her first full view of Behr in the nude.

"Sweet Goddess of the Galaxy. You are gorgeous," she hissed.

Once again, his heated breath sent the thoughts in her head spiraling out of control. She opened her legs when he ran his large hands along the inside of her thighs. Her senses were short-circuiting. The feel of the calluses on his palms intensified the sensation of his touch. His breath was like a torch to kindling, and his skin against hers like a hot blade pressed on soft butter. She wanted to melt around him.

There was no way she could hold back her loud cry when his lips captured the soft nub of her womanhood. She began to shake as he sucked and teased the hidden nub like he did to her nipples. She fought to keep from lowering her arms. She kept her eyes wide open as she blindly stared up at the ceiling of the cabin. Her mind shattered as he ignited a fire in her that was sure to destroy her.

She parted her lips when he slid first one, then two fingers deep inside her channel. He added another finger, stretching her, and she knew he was preparing her for more. She rocked her hips with the movement of his fingers as he thrust them deeper and deeper while he continued to pleasure her clit with his tongue.

She recognized the pressure building inside her. She had experienced it dozens of times since she learned how to pleasure herself. The difference was this time the pressure was magnified a thousandfold. She slid her hands down and cupped her breasts.

"That's it. Play with your nipples. Come for me, Raia. Show me how much you want this," he coaxed.

She pinched her nipples at his command. A low, mewling sound filled the room, building as the pressure inside her grew. With another thrust of his fingers, he sent her over the edge. Raia shuddered with her loud cry of passion as the most intense orgasm she had ever experienced suffused her.

Firm hands gripped her thighs and lifted her hips as she continued to melt in the afterglow of her release. The pressure between her legs changed, and she forced her eyes open. Behr knelt above her, his chest heaving and his face stiff with intense passion.

Raia felt the pressure against her swollen depths channel as he pushed the tip of his cock inside her entrance. Her body opened for him; the slickness of her passionate release eased his way. She stiffened when he reached the barrier that she had never been brave enough to break. She reached up and gripped his forearms when he pushed in deeper. A sharp, intense pain made her catch her breath.

He held himself still. She knew he was waiting for her to show him when she was ready to continue. The discomfort dissipated into a pleasant fullness. She welcomed the sensation of his engorged cock filling her. He stroked her silky channel, and she marveled at his expression of barely controlled passion. A heady sense of feminine power swelled inside her. She wanted him to lose control. She wanted to experience his uncontrolled passionate side.

"Love me, Behr," she said, rocking her hips. "Love me like you mean it."

∼

Love me like you mean it.

Raia's softly spoken words severed the fine thread of control he had managed to keep so far. The taste of Raia's release on his lips, the tightness of her feminine sheath welcoming his throbbing shaft, and the glow of her beautiful face in the dim light of his bedroom would forever be embedded in his mind.

Now, her soft words giving him permission to love her with unadulterated worship snipped the last thread. He cocooned her within his embrace. Pressing his lips against hers, he reveled in pleasure when she raised her legs and pressed her heels against his buttocks.

The move opened her and he took advantage of the new position. He thrust his hips, driving his shaft so deeply that he swore the tip of his cock touched her womb. A shudder ran through him, and he hissed as she moved under him. He could feel every inch of her soft femininity sliding against his blood-engorged shaft.

Her moan of pleasure told him she felt the movement. He rocked his hips in unison with hers. Deepening their kiss, he tangled his tongue with hers. She caressed his body, from his arms to his scarred back.

He groaned, cupped one of her rounded buttocks, and tightened his arms around her as a tingling surged in the base of his spine. Sliding his arms up and under her back, he broke their kiss.

Holding her tightly, he buried his face against the curve of her neck. Their breathing was labored as he thrust into her with increasing speed. Her slick sheath fisted his pistoning shaft, fighting to keep them locked together when he began to withdraw from her. Her low whimpers, pulsing channel, and tight embrace warned him that she was on the verge of another orgasm.

His body reacted when she stiffened and cried out. A sensation of warm moisture coating his cock triggered his orgasm. He thrust forward, his bulbous head flaring and locking them together as he released powerful jets of his semen deep inside her womb.

He threw his head back as he came. The muscles in his arms strained as he fought to keep from crushing her beneath him. For an instant, he couldn't draw a breath. The emotion and intensity of his release was so powerful that it took his breath away.

It took more than a minute for the powerful wave of his release to pass. As it did, he felt weak. His joining with Raia was the most intense experience he'd ever had with a woman.

She released his waist, and pressed a light kiss on his shoulder. She slid her legs down his but kept one of them partially wrapped behind his calf. He leaned back and looked down at her glowing, relaxed face. A slight smile curved her lips, but she kept her eyes closed.

"Wake me when you're ready for round two," she mumbled languidly.

He chuckled and pressed a light kiss on her lips. *I was right. She does glow after a night of lovemaking,* he thought.

He rolled them over so that she was lying on top of his relaxed body. He wrapped his arms around her and rubbed his cheek against the top of her head. A part of him wanted to stay here with her forever—where he knew she would be safe. The other part knew that he couldn't. It was that part that tore at his heart and caused the lone tear to course down his cheek.

CHAPTER TEN

anapare Spaceport

"Have you found anything yet?" Reynar demanded.

Akita stared at her brother's face with a dispassionate expression. Irritation coursed through her. His obsession with Behr De'Mar and the Dregulon had become an interference in her mission.

"You already know the answer, otherwise you wouldn't be asking. I assume He'lo and Orb haven't located them either," she responded in a cool voice.

"No. What is taking you so long?" he snapped.

Akita kept her expression neutral. "I am not one of your minions, Reynar. Unless you have any new information for me, I suggest that you keep your communications to a minimum," she answered.

The heated rage on her brother's face increased. She would not allow him to take his fury out on her. It took him twenty-nine seconds to regain control before he spoke again.

"Notify me when you find something," he said and then ended the communication.

Akita lowered the communication device and slid it into her cloak pocket. She turned around in the narrow maintenance alley that she had stepped into before taking Reynar's summons. At the end of the alleyway, she observed the wealthy patrons strolling along a corridor filled with upscale shops.

While He'lo, Orb, and Reynar were focused on finding Behr and the Dregulon, she was focused on finding information on the two creatures. They would be unusual enough to stand out and be remembered. If she located them, she would locate the Dregulon—and possibly Behr if they were still together. If not, she would at least be able to get a lead on where Behr might be heading.

Adjusting the hood of her expensive, deep purple designer cloak, she pulled on a pair of reflective silver eye shades and topped her disguise with a matching shear scarf. Fortunately, most of the people on Sanapare would be more interested in her clothing than her skin color, and she had covered the only distraction to that—her unusual eyes.

She exited the alley and turned to the right. She surveyed the shops. Clothing, antiquities, bars, and the typical Odds and Ends shops geared for tourists lined each side of the corridor. She narrowed in on a Tiliqua growling threateningly at a group of teens. He scanned the area, his two heads turned in opposite directions, before he retreated into his store.

After walking across the passage to the Tiliqua's store, she entered the dim interior. The typical cheap souvenirs littered the shelves. She had taken only two steps before the shopkeeper was in front of her.

"Welcome to my shop. How can I help you, my lady?" the shopkeeper inquired, his two heads inquired in unison.

"I've lost two of my precious pets and wondered if you might have seen them," Akita replied.

"Do I look like a shop for lost and found?" one of the shopkeeper's heads snapped.

Akita lifted her gloved hand and ran a finger under the chin of the offended head. "What is your name?" she softly inquired.

"F-Frope, my lady," Frope answered.

"Frope," she repeated, sliding her finger down his throat before pulling her hand away. "You've been in business for a while?"

"Y-Yes, nearly forty years," he answered.

She turned away from him and walked along a line of knickknacks. "And you notice everything that goes on," she stated.

"Yes… Well, not everything, but just about everything," he agreed.

"Let's assume for your health and wellbeing that you do see everything, and you might have seen my two missing pets… for a reward, of course," she stated, turning and facing him.

The scowls on the man's faces changed to calculating gleams. For a moment, Akita wondered if a Tiliqua could survive with only one head. One of the man's thick brains must have sensed he was in danger because his right head turned to his left and muttered under his breath.

"Perhaps if you had an image of your missing pet, we could be of assistance—no reward necessary," Frope's right head suggested.

Akita stepped forward and held out a tablet with an image of the two creatures side by side. Frope frowned and mumbled under his breath again. She noticed the Tiliqua's expressions had transformed to anger.

"What do you know?" she encouraged.

"I haven't seen them in a while. They travel with a freighter captain. I recognize the Chumloo. One was stolen from my backroom years ago. The other creature looks just like the one that was with the thief I chased. I lost a lot of credits that day. You don't forget things like that. I know the two stole the Chumloo. The Spaceport authorities did nothing. That's why I have to be vigilant. Some visitors that come here will steal you blind," he grumbled.

"Do you know where the Dregulon is now? Perhaps the name of his ship?" she inquired.

Frope's frown deepened, and he shook his head. "It wasn't a Dregulon. It was some pale-skinned female. She was totally different from the species you usually see around here. The only ones I've ever seen like her live among the Valdier, Sarafin, and Curizan. Maybe they are breeding them," he suggested.

"Are you saying the creatures are traveling with someone other than a Dregulon?" she clarified.

"Yes, that is exactly what I'm saying. The girl never comes in here, but I have noticed her when she visits the antiquities dealer farther down," he replied.

"You have been most helpful, Frope. If anyone asks about the creatures —or the girl, tell them nothing. If I find out that you have talked to anyone about my visit, the creatures, or the girl, I'll return and slit both of your throats. Do you understand?" she asked, lowering her eye shield far enough to reveal her glowing eyes.

Both of Frope's Adam's apples moved up and down as he swallowed nervously. He repeatedly nodded his heads. Confident that the Tiliqua valued both of his necks more than credits, she slid her eye shield back in place and exited the shop.

Now, to visit the antiquities dealer and discover the identity of my Dregulon imposter, she thought.

∽

Planet Raia

. . .

Raia stretched and rolled over, throwing one arm out across the bed. She stared at the ceiling with a slight frown, grinned, and stretched again. Muscles she didn't know she had twinged in protest.

She leaned up on her elbows and looked around. A light shone from the bathroom, but she could see that it was empty. The tantalizing smell of food made her stomach growl.

She sat up and the sheet bunched around her waist. A sound from the doorway drew her attention. Behr leaned against the doorframe. She drew in a swift breath at the expression in his eyes.

"I prepared a meal. Chummy and Pi were vocal about breakfast. It isn't as good as yours, but I think you'll find it edible," he said.

"I'll get cleaned up and be there in a few minutes," she replied.

He remained where he was for a few seconds. Raia grasped the covers as a wave of uncertainty swept through her. The thought that he might regret their lovemaking last night flashed through her mind, and she looked down at the covers.

She swallowed when he sat down on the edge of the bed. Lifting her head, she stared back at him when he caressed her cheek. She met him halfway when he leaned forward to kiss her.

"If it wasn't for Chummy and Pi's insatiable appetites and all the hard work I did preparing a splendid breakfast, I would say to hell with the food and feast on you again," he murmured.

She grinned. "There's always lunch," she teased.

He chuckled and shook his head. "I think I've released a sex monster," he quipped.

He stood and held his hand out to her. She reached out, grasped it, and slid from the bed. His groan sent a shaft of longing through her.

She rested her arms on his shoulders when he cupped her heavy breasts and caressed her tender nipples. A piercing need created a physical pain. She curled her fingers and closed her eyes at the intensity.

"Get cleaned up," he said, kissing her forehead.

When he released her, Raia swayed and opened her eyes. He had turned and was walking out of the room. She lifted her hand and cupped one breast, trying to keep the warmth from his fingers from escaping. From the galley, she heard Behr teasing Chummy and Pi about saving some of the fruit for their mistress.

"Oh, girl. You have it bad," she whispered.

There was no doubt in her mind that she was in love with Behr. The thought both thrilled and scared the hell out of her. How was she supposed to survive when she was with a wanted man hunted by the Marastin Dow military fleet? Unless they stayed here, it was only a matter of time before fleet caught up with them.

No one—not even the Curizan, Sarafin, or Valdier—could save you, I fear.

Evetta's words came back to haunt her. Raia turned and walked into the bathroom. Her thoughts were on all the things that could go wrong if she stayed with Behr, while her body and heart reminded her of all the good things.

How can I let him go? she wondered.

Behr glanced up when Raia entered the galley. He gazed at her greedily. She had pulled her hair into a messy ponytail. Damp, curly tendrils escaped, framing her heart-shaped face. She was wearing a midnight blue tunic tucked into a pair of tan trousers and knee-high boots.

"It smells wonderful," she greeted.

He blinked, forgetting what he was doing. "Yes, well, this is the second attempt. Pi ate my first attempt," he dryly replied.

Pi looked up at him with huge, pitiful eyes, glancing from his face to the pan in his hand and back to his face again. He shook his head and chuckled. The Peekaboo was a bottomless pit.

"Good morning, you two," Raia affectionately greeted, dropping a kiss on Chummy and Pi's heads before sliding onto the seat.

Behr placed a plate of food containing fresh scrambled eggs, sweet bread, and fruit in front of Raia. He waved the ladle in his hand at Chummy and Pi in warning when they eyed Raia's plate. They both sat back in their child seats.

"One more helping and then off you go," he said in a stern tone.

Raia giggled. "You should see my bed. I think they have a month's worth of goodies stashed under it," she said.

He walked back to the table with his plate and two small bowls of fruit on a platter. He set a bowl in front of each animal before he slid in next to Raia. It didn't take long for the two to empty their bowls. He blinked in surprise when Chummy crawled onto the table and over to him. He was about to chide the little Chumloo when Chummy placed a paw on his hand.

Pi say tell her. She will understand, Chummy silently communicated before he scurried off the table and disappeared through the doorway.

He swallowed and stared after Chummy. How the hell did those two always seem to be one step ahead of him? He shook his head in wonder.

"What was that about?" Raia asked.

He sighed. "We have to go back. I have to return," he said, looking at her.

She gave him a wistful smile and looked at her plate. "I know," she softly replied.

"Behr, have you secured the transport?" she called.

"It is locked down," he said from behind her.

Raia nodded and returned to her review of the pre-flight checklist. During the three hours since she had woken up, they had been busy preparing for their departure. They had talked little about the reason. They didn't need to.

"Chummy, are you and Pi ready?" she called.

Chummy ran into the cockpit and looked up at her. *Pi saying bye-bye*.

"Who is she saying bye-bye to?" she asked.

Ghost outside, Chummy answered.

Raia frowned. She shook her head and rose from her seat. She paused when Behr reached out and wrapped his hand around her wrist.

"Is everything alright?" he inquired.

"Yeah, I need to do a visual. I'll be back in a few minutes," she said.

He released her wrist, and she exited the cockpit. She hurried down the corridor to the bay door. Pressing the controller, she impatiently waited for the platform to lower.

She jogged down the ramp and stopped at the end, scanning the area. Cursing under her breath, she was about to yell for Pi when she saw the Peekaboo sitting on the rim of a decorative fountain off beside the plaza. She strode across the expansive space, preparing a stern lecture in her mind as she walked.

"Pi, do you have any idea how close we came to leaving… you?" she said, finishing the question on a whisper of awe.

She slowed to a stop. Sitting on the edge of the fountain with Pi was a woman made of gold. The woman smiled in greeting. Raia resisted rubbing her eyes when the woman transformed in front of her. The woman now resembled the robed Roman figure from the history book Ander had given her—only she wasn't wearing a blindfold.

"Who are you?" she croaked.

"I'm called many things by many species, but you may call me Aminta," she replied in a gentle tone.

"Aminta.... Where did you come from?" Raia demanded.

Aminta rose to her feet, and petted Pi's head. A moment later, Pi disappeared.

"Pi...," Raia said.

"Your very protective friend has returned to the ship. She was worried," Aminta explained.

Raia looked back at the freighter before she returned her attention to Aminta. "What is she worried about?" she asked.

Aminta looked back at her with a gentle expression. "You, Raia," she answered.

"What did she see? What did she show you?" Raia asked in a thick voice.

"The future is not always set in stone," Aminta reflected, running her fingers over a stone sculpture of a fish.

"What is that supposed to mean?" Raia demanded.

Aminta paused. "Sometimes the person you see is not who they really are beneath their exterior. You, yourself, have used a disguise for years to survive. I created this world billions of years ago. Sometimes it seems like yesterday," she mused.

"You created.... Are you saying you are... one of the Goddesses that I've heard about?" Raia asked.

Aminta looked at her and smiled but didn't immediately respond. "There are not as many of us as there once were. Some of my species have lost their way," she murmured.

"Why are you here... now... after all this time? Why haven't I ever seen you before?" Raia asked.

Raia took a step back when Aminta's form shimmered and became more translucent. Aminta gazed around them again. Raia sensed there was something wrong with the woman… Goddess… whatever she was. Aminta sighed.

"Do not be afraid of your destiny, Raia. Behr needs you, but so do the Marastin Dow who wish to break the chains of oppression. Ander knew you were special when he brought you to this star system. Embrace who you are," Aminta said.

"Wait! You can't just leave…," Raia protested as Aminta faded.

"Raia!"

Raia partially turned when she heard Behr's voice. Her gaze was still locked on the spot where Aminta had disappeared. What the hell did Aminta mean?

Don't be afraid of your destiny… embrace who I am?

"This has got to be the most screwed up thing that has ever happened to me," she muttered.

"Raia, are you alright? Pi is on the freighter," Behr said.

"Yeah, I'm alright. I… just thought I saw something," she said with a shake of her head before she turned and gave him a weak smile. "I'm ready now."

They walked back to the freighter in silence. Pi and Chummy sat at the top of the platform, waiting for them. Raia's focus locked on Pi. The little Peekaboo stared back at her with a wide, mischievous look in her eyes. She climbed the ramp.

"You and I need to have a chat later," she said through gritted teeth, slapping her hand on the platform controller.

Goddess is nice, Chummy said.

"I hope so," Raia murmured, searching back across the plaza, hoping to glimpse the elusive Goddess as the platform's hatch sealed.

CHAPTER ELEVEN

Two days later, they emerged from the jump gate into Valdier controlled space, heading for the Kardosa Spaceport. The spaceport hadn't been her initial choice. On the first leg of their journey, they emerged from the jump gate where she had intended to meet up with Mieka and the other Marastin Dow rebel leaders, only to have the *EA II*'s scanners pick up three Marastin Dow warships. They made it to the next jump gate by half a click.

"Are you sure you want to do this? I can think of a half dozen places that would be safer," she said.

"Yes, I'm sure," he replied.

"You realize the place will be crawling with Marastin Dow ships. They may not look like the warships we've seen, but I guarantee they will be there. The insane bastards will attack anything, including a Valdier, Curizan, or Sarafin warship if they can," she said.

He raised an eyebrow at her. "May I remind you I am one of those insane bastards?" he pointed out.

She looked at him and grinned. "I can't imagine how I could have missed that," she teased.

"Hail Mieka. Give her our rendezvous location," he said, rising from his seat.

"I will if you double check with Pi to make sure I'm not taking you to a Spaceport filled with assassins," she called.

"I'll check in with Pi," he promised.

"He better damn well check," she muttered to herself. "I swear, if Pi has one tiny vision of anything happening to him, I'm hightailing it back to Planet Raia."

She pulled up the communications console. "This is the *EA II*, requesting pick up of your cargo," she said.

"This is Chrétien de'Troyes Enterprises. That is good news *EA II*. We were concerned when you were late and didn't communicate your new arrival time. Please confirm your destination for delivery," a smooth voice requested.

Raia closed her eyes and bit her lower lip. She didn't know if her reluctance to answer was due to fear that they were walking into a trap or of her heart breaking. Opening her eyes, she stared at the console.

"Kardosa, usual spot," she replied.

"Confirmed… and thank you, Captain Raia," Mieka replied.

"Arrival expected in six hours," Raia said.

"We'll be ready to receive. Chrétien de'Troyes Entreprises out," Mieka confirmed.

Raia ended the communication and sat back in her seat. Six hours. She had six hours before her heart was ripped to pieces. Reviewing the scanners, she set the autopilot and rose from her seat.

"If I only have six hours, I'm going to make five of them count," she growled under her breath.

∼

Behr sat at the table in the galley, checking each of the weapons Raia had given him. He picked up the portable transporter that Hanine had developed. It was a brilliant piece of technology.

He looked up when he heard footsteps in the corridor. A second later, Raia leaned against the doorframe. She glanced over the array of weapons on the table.

"I've made contact and informed Mieka that you will be at your normal spot. We should arrive in approximately six hours," she said.

He nodded. "Did she say anything else?" he asked.

Raia shook her head. "Only that she was glad you were safe," she replied.

"Thank you again, for everything you've done," he said, sliding out from behind the table and standing.

She shook her head again. "You don't have to thank me. Do you have any idea what you are going to do next? Maradash won't stop looking for you, even if you hide in Valdier, Curizan, or Sarafin controlled space, he'll come after you. I saw the look in his eyes. The man is crazy."

The worry in her eyes made his heart ache. Walking over to her, he slid his arms around her waist and pulled her close. He rested his chin against her head, drawing a deep breath of her scent into his lungs.

"We are so close, Raia. Before I was captured, I discovered information that could change the path of the rebellion. For the past two decades, we've worked to infiltrate the inner workings of the Council. Six of the nine members are old and unwell. They will need to relinquish their positions soon. I discovered a plot by Maradash to eliminate the Council, blame the rebellion, and seize control for himself. He wants to abolish the Council altogether and rule as king. Over the last decade, he has joined forces with a group trying to bring down the Royal families of the Valdier, Curizan, and Sarafin. This is much larger than just our people now, Raia. It is a fight for the entire Star System. If Maradash and whoever he has teamed up with succeed, it will not only mean the end of all hope for my people but for those on every planet in the star system," he explained.

Raia shook her head. "How can that be possible? Since the Valdier, Sarafin, and Curizans have joined forces, they are crazy powerful! Their technology and the sheer size of their military is beyond anything that even Maradash can go up against," she argued.

"My intel says there have been attacks on the three Royal Families. There is supposed to be a weapon strong enough to kill the Valdier's golden creatures. If this intel is true, then the Royal families are in danger. If Maradash attacks them using such a weapon, all Marastin Dow will be blamed and slaughtered. What started as a fight for freedom has now changed into a fight for survival for *all* of us," he quietly added.

Raia pulled back and looked up at him. "Why didn't you tell me this earlier?" she asked.

He caressed her cheek. "Because I was afraid the more you knew, the more danger you would be in," he said.

"What changed your mind?" she asked.

"Pi," he answered.

"What did she show you?" she asked.

"Only that I connect with Mieka and the others," he said.

She lifted her arms and wrapped them around his neck. Arousal hit him hard and fast when he saw the expression in her eyes. The last two days flashed through his mind. There had been little time for them to be together. When they hadn't been running for their lives, they were trying to catch a few hours of rest.

"We have about five hours before we arrive. I would hate to waste them doing nothing," she murmured.

"It would be a terrible waste of time, wouldn't it?" he agreed.

She leaned into him, capturing his lips with hers. Love for her filled him, and he pulled her tightly against his body. He reveled in the passion of her kiss. Needing more, he tugged her shirt free of her trousers and slid his hands up under the thin fabric. He guided her backwards across the corridor and into his cabin without breaking their kiss. Once in his cabin, he lifted the edge of her shirt, and pulled it over her head, barely breaking their kiss.

She fumbled with the fastenings on the front of his shirt. Cool air caressed his heated flesh as she pushed his shirt off his shoulders. She broke their kiss, staring at him with an expression hot enough to melt him to the core. He caught his breath when she moved her hand down to his waist and slid her fingers under the waistband of his pants.

"We still have way too many clothes on," she muttered.

"I think we can take care of that," he replied.

She worked on removing his trousers while he worked on hers. The first time was going to be hot, hard, and fast. They each pulled off their footwear and kicked them and their trousers to the side. His breathing increased when Raia suddenly twisted, pushed him down on the bed, and straddled him.

"I think I'd like to try it on top this time," she murmured.

He lifted his hands and cupped her breasts. His hips instinctively jerked when she wrapped her hand around his throbbing shaft and pumped it. She leaned forward, bracing one hand on his shoulder, and guided his cock toward her silky mound. He uttered a long moan of pleasure when she brushed his bulbous tip against her soft curls.

"Raia, you're playing with fire," he warned.

She leaned forward until her breasts brushed the soft hair on his chest and whispered in his ear. He closed his eyes when a bolt of need, so strong it was a physical pain, speared him.

"I love playing with fire," she whispered.

He slid his hands across her ribs and down, grasping her hips. She released him to grip his shoulders, positioning herself until she was poised above his cock. He thrust upward, parting her protective petals, and pressed deeply into her welcoming heat.

A shudder ran through him. Every inch of his shaft was cocooned tightly within her silky depths. His bulbous head flared in response, stretching her and mixing his pre-cum with hers.

"Behr," she moaned, straightening.

He captured her breasts again, cupping them, and pinched her protruding nipples between his fingers. She leaned into his hands and began to ride him even faster. He met her downward movement with hard thrusts. The combination of their arousal made her passage slick and the friction from their lovemaking created a fire of desire in both of them.

She stiffened and uttered a loud cry as she came. The pulsing of her flesh around his shaft sent a flame of primitive need coursing through him. Lowering his hands to her waist, he slowly lifted her. His body protested the move. The flared head of his cock was not ready to release her.

Raia mewed in protest, her eyes still wild with her release. He rolled her off of him. When she started to open her legs, he shook his head.

"On your knees," he instructed.

She immediately rolled onto her stomach and got up on her knees, ready for him. He climbed up behind her, grasped his aching cock, and found her glistening entrance. The first touch against her almost made him lose control. His cock was so sensitive that he wasn't sure he would last long enough to give her another orgasm.

Gritting his teeth, he pushed into her soft folds. He watched as his cock slid deep inside her. The movement was so beautiful, so erotic, that he wanted to see it again and again until it was burned into his memory.

He held onto her hips and began to move. He slid his shaft in and out, his veins visibly swelling with his desire. Raia clenched the covers of his bed between her fisted hands. Her breasts rocked back and forth with the power of his thrusts.

He didn't stop when she began gasping. Once again, her channel tightened, and he could feel the heat building around his length as he moved in and out of her. The tingling at the base of his spine grew with her cries.

Their orgasms came at the same time while their cries echoed in unison, filling the air. He pressed and held his hips against her buttocks and closed his eyes as he felt the pulsing release of his seed filling her.

He slowly lowered himself over her, caging her beneath him while keeping most of his weight off so he wouldn't crush her. There was no way he could pull out yet. His cock was still too rigid.

He bent his head and kissed the back of her shoulder. Behr closed his eyes when a shudder ran through her as his cock continued to pulse inside her. In response, her inner muscles squeezed him, drawing a low groan out of him in return.

"You are a dangerous woman, Raia Glossman," he muttered.

"You bet your sweet ass I am," she retorted, wiggling her hips a little. "That's two more positions that I could get addicted to. Do you know any others?" she asked.

"I think I can show you a few more before we arrive," he said with a suggestive chuckle.

Raia's stomach knotted as she finished twisting her hair into a knot on the top of her head. In less than an hour, they would reach Kardosa—and she would be saying goodbye to Behr. Tears burned her eyes at the thought of never seeing him again, and one stubborn droplet escaped. She impatiently wiped it away.

"You knew this was going to happen. Deal with it. He has bigger things than you to worry about," she mumbled.

"Warning. Incoming spaceships detected," the ship's computer announced.

"I know, I know," she growled.

She stepped out of Behr's cabin only to stumble back, grabbing the doorframe to keep from falling when Pi rolled by. Shaking her head, she stepped out again—and straight into a floating Chummy. She reached up and grabbed the Chumloo around his stomach.

We get to explore? Chummy asked.

"Yes, but only after our business there is done," she stated.

Pi know good place to eat, Chummy said.

Raia sighed and cuddled Chummy in her arms. "Pi *always* knows where the best places to eat are," she dryly retorted.

Chummy snuggled against her as she carried him to the cockpit of the freighter. Behr rose and moved from the pilot to the co-pilot seat. Raia handed Chummy to him.

"Pi is already planning her next meal," Behr informed her.

"Isn't she always?" Raia replied. "Kardosa Control, this is the *Explorer Adventure II* requesting permission to dock."

"*Explorer Adventure II*, welcome to Kardosa Spaceport. You are cleared to dock on Level 8, Bay 20," the controller replied.

"Acknowledged Level 8, Bay 20. Thank you, Clem," she replied.

"Happy to see you back, Raia. Please be advised that there is an MPA parasite warning in effect," Clem added.

Raia blew out a breath. "Acknowledged. I'll avoid contamination if possible. *EA II* out," she answered.

"I don't think I've ever heard of an MPA parasite before. What is that?" Behr asked.

Raia maneuvered the freighter around a slower one and held her position as two supply ships launched. She carefully studied the different levels, noting the assorted ship models. Most of the ships she recognized from her various travels through the star system. There were four that she didn't, and one in particular that stood out.

"Raia, what is it?" he asked.

"What? Oh, nothing. Clem has been with Kardosa control forever. He was a good friend of Ander's. When I first started hauling, he took me aside and told me he and Ander had made up codes to kind of watch each other's back. MPA stands for Major Pain in the Ass. That means Valdier inspectors or military are here," she explained. "Since I'm not carrying any illegal cargo—well, except for you—I'll be fine. I'm going to give you the personal hologram device Hanine made for me. You still have three assassins looking for you, not to mention that I wouldn't put it past Maradash to offer a price that every bounty hunter in the star system will be itching to cash in on," she said.

"What about you? Won't you need it?" he asked.

She shook her head. "I'll get Hanine to make me another one. Besides, no one is chasing me. They are too busy looking for a Dregulon," she replied.

"Thank the Goddess for that," he murmured.

"*Explorer Adventure II*, this is Valdier Military Security. Prepare for inspection," a deep voice ordered.

Raia groaned and looked at Behr. "*Explorer Adventure II* acknowledged. Give me ten minutes to shut down and decompress the air lock," she said before cutting the transmission. "It looks like you'll get to test out your disguise sooner than we expected. What would you like to be? And the bigger question—male or female?" she inquired with a wry grin.

CHAPTER TWELVE

"Who is this?" the Valdier warrior demanded.

"My great-aunt's sister's cousin on my mother's side. Who do you think she is? She's a paying guest looking to start a business on Kardosa," Raia sarcastically replied.

The man glared at his companion when he chuckled. "Do you have anything you need to declare?" he requested.

"Yes, I had the best sex of my life less than an hour ago, and you are totally blowing the afterglow," she remarked. She peered at the screen he was holding. "That is totally with two l's."

The warrior glared at her before turning to look at her companion. "Is she always this… difficult?" he asked, looking at the tall, stately Tearnat woman sitting at the table.

"Yes. Is there anything else you need?" the woman replied.

"No, that will be all. Enjoy your stay," the warrior grumbled before pushing past his companion and heading toward the side exit of the ship.

"You know, she looks a lot like the Dragon Lords' mates. I heard that

Prince Mandra's mate once knocked him out with a flowerpot," the second warrior was saying with wonder as they departed.

Raia folded her arms over her chest and grinned at the woman glaring at her across the table. "I told you it would work," she said.

"Really? You couldn't have programmed something a little different?" Behr demanded in a high voice.

Raia giggled. "You were too tall for the Tiliqua image. It was either the Gelatian or the Tearnat. There aren't many of them, and Hanine hasn't programmed a slime trail for the Gelatian yet. That would be a dead giveaway that you aren't who you look like. A wealthy Tearnat looking to open a business is the perfect cover. Being a woman is even better—plus, you'll get to see all the crap women have to put up with. Besides, I think you look amazing in that designer outfit with the slit showing off your green, scaly legs," she said with a grin.

He walked forward and kissed her lips. "You have a very strange sense of humor," he muttered.

She laughed and slapped him on the ass. The computerized version of him reacted to the contact, and his tail swished. His tail looked so real that she started to jump away before she remembered and the holographic image passed through her legs.

"We'd better go before I change my mind, kidnap you, and take you back to Planet Raia where I'll keep you as my sex slave," she said.

Behr raised his hand and caressed her cheek when her voice cracked on the last two words. She was trying to keep it together, but inside it felt like she was falling apart. It didn't help that she couldn't see Behr's face behind the illusion of the Tearnat.

"Promise me you'll stay safe," she whispered.

"I wish I could. Raia...," he said before he stopped and shook his head. "We'd better go."

She swallowed and nodded. Turning away, she stepped out into the corridor. Tears were threatening to blind her.

"Chummy, Pi, time to go," she called in a thick voice.

Chummy and Pi peered around the corner of her cabin door. They had been hiding, staying one step ahead, while the Valdier searched her freighter. Now the two squealed with delight and burst from her room, going ahead of them. Their enthusiasm caused her to laugh.

"Pay attention and don't get caught," she called when they disappeared ahead of her.

"Will they be alright?" Behr asked with concern.

"Pi will keep them safe. She'll know if there is danger and can pop them back here in a heartbeat," she said. "Do you have all the things I gave you?"

"Yes. I worry that I'm taking things you will need," he confessed.

She gave him a strained smile and shook her head. "It's okay. I think I'll go visit Ben and Evetta for a few weeks after… after I leave here. I haven't been by in months. It'll be good to see Bennie and Nayua again," she said.

"Raia, I wish…," he began.

She turned and put her fingers against his lips. "No regrets. Promise me you won't have any regrets," she said.

"I promise," he repeated.

She gave him a sharp nod. They walked along the long corridor until they reached the lifts leading into the Spaceport. They stepped inside and Behr requested Level 10. They exited at the same time, but Raia went to the left while Behr moved to the right.

She would meet up with Mieka and assess the situation. Once they felt it was safe, she would leave, and Behr would join Mieka and the others.

Then we'll both disappear, she thought.

She flexed her fingers, trying to control the emotions raging inside her. Her heart was breaking. She could feel it shattering into a billion pieces. Other patrons must have sensed her distress, and she knew if she didn't get her emotions under control that she could endanger Behr and his comrades.

Stepping into a service alley, she leaned back against a wall and breathed deeply, trying to calm the ache in her heart. The pain of losing Behr felt more intense than she remembered when she had lost Ander. She lowered her head and looked at her hands. They were shaking.

"I have to be strong. I can't fall apart. If I do, I could endanger him. I have to be strong. I have to be strong," she whispered.

She whispered the words over and over until she felt she was back in control. Taking a deep, shuddering breath, she straightened her shoulders, shook her head to clear it, and forced an emotionless mask onto her face. She had a job to do, and she would do it, even if it killed her.

Feeling calmer, she stepped out of the alley and continued on her way. She weaved in and out of the pedestrians. Ahead of her was an open-air bar. Sitting at a table near one of the tall support pillars were two Chazen Desert Dwellers.

Raia pushed her way between two men blocking the entrance. She looked down when one of the men grabbed her arm. She returned the man's beady-eyed stare with one of her own.

"*Ta sheba nu ebba,*" 'Let go of my arm,' she ordered.

The two men chuckled. "*Kabi moi,*" 'Make me,' he replied.

Out of the corner of her eye, she saw one of the Chazen partially rise out of his seat. Behind him, she could see Behr. He had entered through the rear entrance. She shook her head when he started threading his way through the crowded tables.

"*Sabi lie one ebbi eno poof,*" 'You have one minute before it explodes,' she replied, pulling the front of the man's pants forward just far enough to drop a small cylinder inside.

The man released her with a yelp and jumped away, grabbing for his crotch. The other man was asking him what was wrong. The man who had grabbed her hissed that she had placed an explosive in his pants. The moment he shared that information, the second man backed away and disappeared into the crowd.

"*Shenawa itc,*" 'She bitch,' the man snarled.

He pushed his way past her and headed to the restroom. Some patrons snickered while others yelled at him. He ignored everyone. He was too busy groping the front of his pants to care. Raia lifted her chin and smirked when he paled, stumbled, and fell to the ground in a whimpering heap.

"What did you do to him?" the Chazen asked.

Raia recognized Mieka's voice. "A neat little device a friend came up with that releases a burn powder. He'll feel like his balls are on fire and fear they are going to fall off for a few days. If he's smart, he won't ever wear those pants again because the stuff doesn't wash out," she replied.

"You are as resourceful as I've heard," Mieka said with a chuckle.

"I've had to learn to be," Raia replied.

"Do you have the package?" Mieka quietly inquired as they walked back to her table.

Raia's heart twisted with anguish. For a moment, she forgot the real reason why she was here. It would be so easy to lose herself in the delusion that this was all make-believe.

"Yes, he is here," she replied.

"Where?" Mieka asked, scanning the patrons.

"Close enough to hear what you are saying," Raia replied.

Mieka frowned, and her partner looked around. Out of the corner of her eye, she saw Behr raise a drink in their direction. Mieka's eyes widened with surprise, and she turned around, looking at Raia for confirmation.

"A Tearnat female?" Mieka hissed, trying not to chuckle.

Raia gave the other woman a strained smile. "Let's just say I'm better with costumes than you are," she replied.

Mieka looked back at Behr. Raia waited to see what would happen next. Finally, the woman turned and nodded to the man next to her. He reached into his pocket, pulled out a bag, and slid it across the table to her. She took the bag without looking inside.

"Don't you want to confirm that we paid you?" Marus asked.

Raia shook her head. "I trust you," she quietly said.

Mieka tilted her head and stared back at her. Raia looked away. She didn't enjoy seeing her wounded expression reflected in the goggles the other woman was wearing. She rose to her feet.

"Please tell Behr to be more careful in the future. It wasn't easy breaking his ass out of that prison. I don't think Maradash would give him a chance to do it again," she instructed in a thick voice before she turned and walked away.

Pain gripped her, tearing at her insides until she feared she would be sick. She wrapped her hand around the bag of credits and shoved it into the pocket of her jacket. She felt like she couldn't breathe. Pulling her hood up, she bowed her head and headed for the lifts. She needed to find Chummy and Pi and get out of here—now.

Akita sat at the table of the café along the main corridor on Level 5. She had arrived at the Kardosa Spaceport two days ago after intercepting a message about a freighter that had eluded two Marastin Dow warships. The freighter had made a jump. Out of the three locations where the ship could go from that jump gate, this one made the most sense. It was the only one where safety came in the form of Valdier warships.

The dragon-shifters had been riled up since the attacks on the Royal family. Her lip curled when one of the warriors walked past her with an appreciative expression. His dragon must not have felt the same way given the startled expression that flashed across his face before it twisted into a look of disgust.

Obviously, he doesn't care for purple-skinned assassins, she mused.

A movement in the shadows across from her drew her attention. She turned and focused her attention on the corner where a merchant had set up a table of fresh fruits and nuts. The cloth covering the table moved again.

She smiled when she saw two heat signatures. Blinking, she captured the image in a retina picture and sent it to her scanner. Looking down, she studied the picture of the two small creatures. Both matched the images from the prison.

"Now, where is your mistress?" she murmured.

She wasn't interested in the animals. They could do what they wanted. No, she wanted their mistress.

Akita soon found herself surprisingly enthralled by the antics of the two animals. The tan and white one would suddenly appear when no one was looking and drop a piece of fruit over the side of the table. Akita would follow the movement of the fruit only to lose track of the tan and white creature who would miraculously appear at a different table. The plump, black and white creature would dart between the tables and catch the fruit before it hit the ground.

What fascinated her most was that the tan and white creature would drop a credit in the spot where it had taken fruit. Even with her enhanced skills, she could not keep up with them. She was concerned that they might escape before their mistress arrived.

She half rose from her seat only to sink back down when she noticed a hooded figure approaching the fruit stand. The jacket was open in front, revealing that the person was a woman. Pale hands rose, and the woman slid the hood of her jacket back, revealing her face.

Success, Akita thought with satisfaction.

Akita's gaze followed Raia as she walked around the table. Raia shook her head when the merchant asked if she needed assistance. Akita rose and moved along the street, keeping Raia within sight.

She paused outside a store and watched in the reflective glass as Raia knelt down and pulled something from her jacket. Both creatures nodded. Raia took the fruit they had pilfered, exchanging a small black bag for the succulent fruit.

In the blink of an eye, the creatures disappeared. Akita remained where she was, watching Raia stand in the alley for several minutes. She watched the woman's movements as she tucked the fruit into another bag that she pulled from her jacket. Finally, Raia pulled the jacket hood back up before she stepped into the crowded street.

Akita's smile of satisfaction faded when she noticed two familiar dark shapes following Raia. It would appear that the Tiliqua wasn't as good at keeping his word as he had promised.

Raia lifted her hand and rubbed her cheek. It didn't matter how many times she wiped the tears away, they just kept falling. Frustrated, she pulled her portable communicator out of her pocket. She muttered an apology when she bumped into someone in her distraction. Biting her lip, she lifted the device before she cursed and shoved it back into her pocket.

"What am I going to say? Hey, Evetta. Do you or Hanine have a device that can fix a broken heart? No? Can you make one?" she mumbled. "If I did that, I'd have all four of them coming here and endangering themselves. I don't know what's worse, the idea of putting them in harm's way or leaving Bennie home alone while they do!"

She sniffed loudly and headed for the lifts. If she left now, she could be on Ceran-Pax by the end of the week. She had enough credits to cover her expenses for the next year if she was careful. The transport they had brought back from Planet Raia should be enough of a distraction to keep Evetta and Hanine from driving her crazy with questions. Ben… well, he was a different story. There would be no escaping his intense scrutiny.

"You don't look like a Dregulon to me," a deep, scratchy voice growled behind her.

Raia wheeled around and stumbled backwards. Lost in her dismal thoughts, she had left the crowded streets and turned into the quieter terminal leading to the docking bays. She swallowed hard when she recognized the two men standing before her. They were the two assassins from the files Mieka had sent her and Behr.

"I'm sorry, you have the wrong person. As you can see, I'm not a Dregulon," she stated.

"Where is De'Mar?" the man named Orb demanded.

Raia lifted an eyebrow and stared back at him. "De'Mar… never heard of him. Have you checked the bars? That's usually the first place most people go when they arrive," she suggested.

"You think you are so smart," the Triloug, He'lo, growled.

Raia shrugged. "I did alright with my studies. I wasn't at the top of my classes, but I wasn't at the bottom either. Well, come to think of it, I was the top and the bottom since I was the only one in my class," she replied with a sardonic smirk.

She stiffened when Orb lifted a blade and flashed it at her. Perhaps antagonizing them wasn't the best option. She hoped that if she delayed them long enough, Clem would get around to watching the damned surveillance footage and notify the Valdier. The only time she wanted a dragon-shifting warrior bothering her, and they were too busy patrolling freighters!

He'lo held his arm out when Orb took a step toward her. "Maradash wants her alive," he reminded Orb.

Orb's tusks moved up and down in agitation. "She can be alive without her tongue," he snapped.

"She needs to talk. If you cut her tongue out, she won't be able to tell Maradash where De'Mar is," He'lo retorted.

"She can draw him a map," Orb sneered.

Raia backed up a step and shook her head. "Bottom of the class, remember? I'm really hopeless when it comes to drawing and directions," she said, feeling behind her for the summons button to the lift.

"You a Captain, ain't you?" Orb snorted. "She's lying. I'll cut her lying tongue out and give it to Maradash. If he wants, he can have one of his fancy scientists sew it back on like they did his sister's eyes. Maradash didn't say nothing about keeping her in one piece. I'll make sure she lives—long enough to get there."

"I'm afraid it doesn't quite work that way," a woman coolly stated.

Both men turned at once. Raia's eyes widened when they both attacked the woman at the same time. Raia recognized the woman as the third assassin.

Akita moved with the grace of a dancer as she parried strikes from the men's blades with two foot-long blades. She twirled, slicing a blade across the belly of the Triloug. The man roared with outrage.

Raia pushed on the lift summons button several times. She was trapped between three assassins and the lift in a triangular alcove. Every time she tried to slip past them, one would get in her way. All she could do was try to stay out of the way of the sharp blades.

She barely ducked quickly enough when Orb's blade suddenly extended and became a long chain of razor-sharp blades that could take a limb off with a single swipe. The whip-like blade zipped by her again, and she was forced to roll across to the other side of the alcove.

The chain swept out toward Akita. Raia was sure the woman was dead. Instead, the woman caught the chain between two links with her short swords and did a midair flip. When she landed, she was crouching between Raia and the lift door. He'lo stood in the middle with Orb on the other side, struggling to pull the chain back.

Akita lowered her short blades, releasing the chain. It snapped back, cleanly slicing through He'lo in a vertical cut that parted the man down the middle. Orb stumbled back from the force of the whiplash just as the lift chimed.

Raia stepped into the lift the moment the doors opened. Akita followed her, backing up and keeping her eyes locked on Orb who was struggling to regain his balance. He straightened as the doors began to close and raised his arm.

"Look out," Raia called out with alarm.

She didn't know why she did what she did. It could have been out of reflex, just plain craziness, or an unconscious death wish. Whatever the reason, she regretted it the moment she shoved Akita aside, out of danger, just as Orb fired his laser pistol.

Raia stumbled back against the wall of the lift and stared at Akita in disbelief. Her hand pressed against the burning pain spreading through her lower abdomen. She looked down at her hand when warm red liquid began to seep through her fingers.

Her head fell back, and she started to slide down the lift wall. Surprise filled her when Akita wrapped her arm around Raia's waist and stared at her with her strange, glowing eyes. Raia tilted her head back.

"You have the coolest, most beautiful eyes," Raia whispered.

Akita's hold around her waist tightened, keeping her up, and she shook her head. "You are a very, very strange woman," the assassin muttered.

Raia gave Akita a weak smile. "Yeah, that's what I've been told," she muttered.

"Who told you that?" Akita asked.

Raia shook her head. Akita's voice sounded like it was in an echo chamber. Why was the assassin holding her up? Why was it so cold in here?

"Raia, who told you that?" Akita demanded.

Raia closed her eyes, and she began to cry. Akita lowered her to the floor of the lift. Raia turned her head away from the woman.

"Who told you that?" Akita repeated in a gentle voice.

"I love him, and I'll never see him again. Why does that hurt more than being shot? Why? Why does it hurt so much?" Raia whispered, opening her eyes and letting all her pain show.

Akita shook her head. "I don't know," she replied.

Raia turned her head away. Looking down, she could see He'lo's dismembered body in a pool of blood. Orb had vanished and a small crowd was gathering. The two Valdier warriors who had boarded her freighter earlier were at the scene. The thought that Clem must have finally looked at the video feed struck her as funny.

The last thing she saw was a small group off to the side. Two people dressed as Chazen Desert Dwellers—and a female Tearnat. She forced her hand up to the glass and splayed it. Her lips moved, but no sound emerged.

I love you, she silently mouthed as darkness descended around her, and her hand fell limply to the floor.

CHAPTER THIRTEEN

*B*ehr shrugged off Mieka's restraining hand when Pi and Chummy suddenly appeared before them as they made their way along a service alley. He knelt when the two creatures ran up to him. Chummy placed a tiny paw on his hand.

Raia need help, Chummy said.

"Behr, what is it?" Mieka asked.

"Raia," he replied. "Pi, show me."

Pi wrapped her tiny hand around his outstretched index finger. Images of Raia slumped in the lift filled his mind. His breath hissed out when he saw Akita's face. Pulling his hand free, he rose and turned.

"Where are you going? The ship is the other way," Mieka protested.

"Raia is in danger," he said.

Mieka reached out and gripped his arm. "It could be a trap," she warned.

"It probably is," he impatiently replied.

Mieka's grip tightened on his arm when he tried to pull away. "She knew the risk. Let her go, Behr. There is more at stake from the little you've told me," she reminded him.

A muscle twitched in his jaw. He looked down at Chummy and Pi. They stared at him with large, soulful eyes. Pi reached over and wrapped her tiny arms around the Chumloo. In a flash, they disappeared.

"I can't let her go," he said in a low voice.

He pulled free of Mieka's grasp and retraced his steps back to the main corridor. Behind him, he heard Marus curse under his breath, and the sound of footsteps hurrying to catch up with him. Turning to the right, he broke into a run. The vision had shown the lifts going back to the freighter.

The sound of a distant, horrified scream sent a flood of adrenaline through him. He pushed through the crowd of curious pedestrians who stopped and faced the direction the scream had come from before they continued on their way. His heart raced as he ran down the corridor to the lift station.

"Be careful!"

Mieka's breathless warning pierced his mind, and he slowed down when he saw a group of bystanders clustered ahead of him. A man plowed into Behr, almost knocking him off his feet. His breath hissed out when he recognized the man. Orb ran past Mieka and Marus and disappeared down a service alley.

"Behr, look!" Marus said, staring up at the rising lift.

Behr followed Marus's gaze. He clenched his jaw when he saw Akita standing in the lift. Another movement inside the lift pulled his attention lower, and a guttural cry of denial broke from his lips. He stared at Raia's crumpled figure leaning against the glass.

"Raia…," he hoarsely whispered.

"You were supposed to notify me the moment you found something. Orb said that it was a woman disguised as a Dregulon who broke De'Mar out," Reynar snapped.

Akita sat back in her seat and stared at her brother. "Did he also tell you he killed her? I was following her to De'Mar. He'lo and Orb got in the way," she said.

"Can no one do anything right? Do I have to do everything myself?" he replied.

She raised an eyebrow, studied his scarred cheek, but refrained from mentioning that De'Mar had slipped out from under his nose in the first place. There was no sense in antagonizing Reynar. He would only kill someone.

"Do you have any leads on De'Mar's location?" he asked.

"No. The woman was alone when she arrived. De'Mar must have disembarked earlier," she replied.

"What about the logs from her navigation system? Have you accessed them?" he demanded.

"Yes," she responded.

Irritation flashed through his eyes. "And…?" he growled.

"And… they are garbage. They have her on Ceran-Pax getting repairs for the last three months. Unless she used a different ship, the records are inaccurate," she replied.

"Orb said you killed He'lo and that you were defending the woman," Reynar said.

Akita lifted an eyebrow at his suspicious tone. "You were very clear that you wanted De'Mar and the one who helped him escape brought back alive. He'lo already stopped Orb from killing her once before I made my presence known. They turned and tried to kill me. Of course I reciprocated. They were sloppy, brother. Now the Valdier are on high alert. It is known that He'lo worked for you. I barely escaped before they arrived," she bit out.

"What are your plans?" he asked.

"Why, to clean up your mess, brother," she said with a saccharine smile that didn't reach her eyes.

She reached out and cut off the transmission before Reynar's furious retort could be voiced. Tapping the arm of her chair with her fingers, she contemplated her next move. Orb would come after her.

"Computer, set a course for Ceran-Pax," she instructed.

Rising from her seat, she exited the cockpit of the Edge military spacecraft she had commissioned. The controller she was wearing on her wrist vibrated with an alert. A slight smile curved her lips.

"Excellent," she said.

Raia forced her eyes open. At the moment, the simple task felt like a monumental one. She lifted her right hand and touched her stomach.

"You need to stay in the regenerator for at least another hour or two."

Raia swallowed and turned her head to the side. Akita stood in the doorway, watching her. She swallowed, unsure of what to say.

"Hi," she mumbled.

That probably wasn't the smartest thing to say to an assassin, she thought with a mental wince, and closed her eyes.

Akita's chuckle made her open her eyes, and she stared at the woman. Raia warily waited as the woman crossed the room and stood next to her. Akita read the computer report that the medic system was generating.

"Why did you save my life?" Akita asked, staring down at her.

Raia tried to shrug, but it took too much effort. Instead, she wiggled her nose. It was the best she could do at the moment.

"Bad reflexes," she quipped.

Akita chuckled again. "Are your species born without an ounce of survival instincts, or is it just you?" she inquired.

"Ouch, that was a little blunt," Raia said with a roll of her eyes. She turned her head and stared up at the ceiling. "Can I ask a few questions?"

"Yes."

Akita's answer surprised her, and she looked at the woman again. "Are you going to kill me?" she asked in a low voice.

Akita appeared to think about the question before she answered. "Not at this moment," she replied.

"Okay, question number two. Are you going to let me go?" she asked.

"Not at this moment," Akita repeated with a slight smile.

Raia sighed. "Can you tell me what is going on?" she requested.

Akita smiled. "Not…," she began.

"… At this moment," Raia finished with a heavy sigh. "So, what am I supposed to do… or not do? Can you at least tell me that at this moment?" Raia demanded in a frustrated voice.

"Heal. Then, I will make a decision," Akita said, turning away from her.

"Akita… why did you save me?" Raia softly called.

Akita paused in the doorway. Raia waited. After a few seconds, the assassin walked out of the door without saying anything.

Raia turned her head and stared up at the ceiling again. She thought of Behr. He probably thought she was dead. A tear slid from the corner of her eye.

"Perhaps that's for the best," she whispered, closing her eyes again as pain from her broken heart washed through her.

"Behr, this is madness. You saw the vidcoms. Raia is dead. If the injury from Orb didn't kill her, Akita would have finished the job," Marus stated.

"If you don't want to be here, you can transfer back to the *Traitor's Run*," he snapped.

"Nonsense. If I did that, Mieka would probably eject me into space… without a suit," Marus grunted.

"Then help me find her," he quietly asked.

"Why is she so important? From what you've shared, there are far more urgent matters that need to be addressed than chasing a half-dead woman and an assassin across the star system," Marus said.

"She found the Marastin Dow home world," Behr replied.

"Of course she knows where Spardonian is, she rescued you from the prison there," Marus impatiently said.

"I'm not talking about Spardonian. I'm talking about Empyrean," Behr said.

Marus stared at him as if he had gone mad. "*She… knows where Empyrean is located?*" he mumbled in awe.

Behr nodded. "Yes. Not only that, I've been there, Marus," he said, pausing in his pre-flight check to look at the other man.

"You've been—" Marus's voice faded, and he shook his head. "I always believed it was a myth."

"So did I," he said as he uttered a short, low laugh. Marus raised an eyebrow in inquiry. He shook his head. "She calls it Planet Raia."

Emotion threatened to overwhelm him when he remembered the sight of her laughing, excited face that first day in the plaza. He ground his teeth together and pushed the memory away.

She was alive. She had to be. The universe couldn't lose someone whose soul burned as brightly as a star.

"This is the *Explorer Adventure II* requesting permission to depart," he stated.

"The *EA II* is Raia's ship. Who are you?" the controller demanded.

"I'm the man who loves her," he replied.

There was a brief silence before Clem replied. "*Explorer Adventure II*, you are cleared for departure. If that girl is alive, you go find her and save her," Clem ordered.

"Acknowledged," Behr responded in a tight voice.

Marus looked at him. "How will we find her?" he asked.

"Take over. Take us out of range of the Spaceport, but keep us within the Valdier controlled shipping lanes," he instructed, turning the controls over to Marus.

"Where are you going?" Marus asked.

Behr rose from his seat. "To talk to a furry friend," he replied.

Behr walked down the corridor to Raia's cabin. He paused in the open doorway and looked around. This was the first time he had been inside her quarters. They had stayed in his cabin when they were together.

He closed his eyes and gripped the doorframe as another wave of anguish struck him. There was so much about Raia he still didn't know

—and might never find out. He opened his eyes and scanned the interior.

Raia had built a bookcase into the wall farthest from the door. Knick-knacks and books she had collected lined the shelves, giving the small space a personalized touch. An old book lay open on the corner desk, and tiny crystals hung from the ceiling, glowing like miniature stars. The room looked as if Raia had just stepped out for a moment. He slowly entered, wishing he had more time to explore.

"Pi," he called in a low voice.

He listened. The sound of a whimper came from somewhere near Raia's bed. He remembered Raia telling him that the two creatures had made a home for their treasures underneath it. He walked over to the bed and sat down.

"Pi, I need your help to find Raia," he said.

The sound of movement under the bed confirmed his suspicions. He moved his foot aside when he spotted the edge of a bright red fluffy pillow being pushed out from under the bed. Chummy was the first one to emerge.

Behr's face softened when Chummy and the pillow floated up to the bed. He reached out and caressed the Chumloo's head. A nudge on his elbow startled him. Pi had appeared behind him and was trying to climb onto his lap.

He lifted his arm so the little Peekaboo could crawl onto his lap. Pi rubbed her head against his chest. He wrapped his arm around her while he continued to pet Chummy.

"Pi, I need to know…." He paused and drew in a deep, steadying breath before he continued. "Pi, I need to know where Raia is."

Raia bye-bye, Chummy mewed.

"Yes, Raia is bye-bye. I need to know where she is so we can go get her," he said.

Pi stretched up and placed her tiny hands on each side of his face. He stared into the Peekaboo's eyes. He saw his reflection there—and then he saw so much more. He caught his breath at the vivid pictures playing like a vidcom in his mind.

His eyes filled with tears as he became lost in the moving images of Raia's life through Pi's eyes. The slender young girl in the alley with kind eyes and a gentle touch. Raia laying on her bed night after night, reading stories to her two friends. Raia laughing as she made their dinner. Baths, running through fields, visiting the spaceports, celebrating special moments, all of Pi's memories of Raia flooded him like a tidal wave.

He drew in a shaky breath when Pi showed him a snapshot of him and Raia wound around each other in his bed. Raia's hair was spread out across the pillow. Her eyelashes lay against her cheeks like two crescent moons, and her soft, pink lips were parted as she slept. She was lying on her side with her hands over his as he lay curled around her.

You… bring our Raia home? Chummy pleaded.

"Yes, I will bring Raia home," he murmured.

You no leave us? Chummy asked.

Behr gently shook his head. "No, I won't leave you," he promised.

The vision Pi was showing him changed, and he saw Akita holding a blade to Raia's throat. Six people stood in front of them. He recognized four of them. The vision faded, and Pi crawled off his lap and snuggled against Chummy.

Behr rose to his feet. He looked at Chummy and Pi. He rubbed a hand under his eye, clenching his fist when he felt a slight dampness, and nodded.

"Thank you," he murmured.

Turning, he exited the cabin and strode back to the freighter's cockpit. He slid into the pilot seat and reached for the navigation controls. Marus waited and watched.

"Ceran-Pax," Marus noted with a curious expression.

"Yes. Raia's alive. She is on Ceran-Pax… and so is Akita," he added in a grim tone.

CHAPTER FOURTEEN

*R*aia sat back in the co-pilot seat and moodily stared out the front windshield. She grimaced when a strand of her wavy hair fell across her face and she had to lift both hands to brush it back thanks to the wrist cuffs.

"You realize that these things really aren't necessary. It's not like there is anywhere I can go," she muttered.

Akita ignored her—just like she had been ignoring her ever since she emerged from the regenerator. Raia leaned her head back, stared up at the ceiling of the Marastin Dow space ship, and groaned.

Being a prisoner sucks, she thought.

"Do you need to visit the regenerator again?" Akita inquired.

"No, I need to move. I'm not used to sitting around wearing wrist cuffs and being bored out of my mind," she complained.

"It makes no sense to release you," Akita replied.

"Why? Are you afraid I might steal your bed linens or Tirrella crystals? Okay, I might do that, but what if I promise not to?" she offered, flopping her head forward and glaring at Akita.

Akita gave her a pointed glare. "I have killed less irritating creatures than you for sport. If I released you, you might attack me," she reasoned.

Raia shook her head. "Listen, I might be a lot of things… fantastic things, I might point out… but being too stupid to live is not one of them. Why would I want to attack a Marastin Dow, much less a *trained assassin* Marastin Dow… on a ship… where I can't escape?" she pointed out.

"I am not releasing you. If you don't shut up, I will knock you out," Akita warned.

Raia pursed her lips. Obviously irritating the woman wasn't going to work. The edge in Akita's voice made Raia believe that while the assassin might not kill her, she would definitely follow through with her threat. Tapping her fingers on her knees, she pondered what else she could do when a planet came into view.

Raia swung her legs over the arm of the chair and sat up. She parted her lips on a protest. They were heading to Ceran-Pax.

"Why… why are we going here?" she asked in a voice that wasn't quite steady.

"It is where the people you care about live," Akita coolly replied.

"Yes, but… why?" she asked.

Anger mixed with her fear. Her mind raced as she tried to second-guess Akita. All the end possibilities she contemplated made her sick to her stomach.

"Did you think that once I found out about you, I wouldn't find out about the two traitors and their mates? You will tell me everything Behr De'Mar told you, or you will watch your family die," Akita threatened.

"They are under the protection of the Curizan Prince Ha'ven Ha'darra. They can't help you. They live on a farm and have stayed away from the Marastin Dow," she protested.

"They are traitors and were sentenced to be executed for their crimes. You will tell me where De'Mar is," Akita said.

"I can't tell you," she muttered, closing her eyes and bowing her head.

"Can't… or won't?" Akita retorted.

Raia lifted her head and glared at the woman. "I can't because I don't know. If I did, then it would be won't," she snapped.

Akita turned and looked at her with an assessing look. Raia returned the woman's stare with one of her own. She refused to let Akita intimidate her.

"You love him," Akita murmured.

Raia stiffened and lifted her chin. "I don't know what you're talking about," she stubbornly retorted.

Akita's lips curved into a sly smile. "Behr De'Mar. You love him. You said that you did in the lift," she added.

Raia swallowed and resisted the urge to look away. "I never said I was in love with De'Mar. I could have been talking about someone else," she defended.

Akita chuckled and looked out the front windshield at the fast-approaching planet. "You could have been, but you weren't. I don't think it will be necessary for me to find him after all," she said.

Raia frowned. "Why do you say that? Are you giving up?" she asked.

Akita shook her head. "No. He will come for you. He was there at the Spaceport. He saw He'lo… and possibly me. He'll conclude I have you when your body isn't found. He'll come," she said.

"No, he won't. He thinks I'm dead. If not, it wouldn't matter, anyway. What he is fighting for is far bigger than me," she murmured.

Akita was silent for a moment before she spoke. "I hope not," she said.

Raia wasn't sure what Akita meant by that. She sat back in her seat. Her gaze fixed on Ceran-Pax. It was a big planet. Surely Akita couldn't know about the obscure refugee village nestled between two large mountain ranges.

Her hope began to fade when Akita turned to the northeast. She fervently scanned the outer perimeter of the planet, searching for a Curizan patrol ship. She always saw one when she arrived and departed.

"Freighter 225, you are cleared for entry," a voice stated.

"Freighter 225 acknowledges clearance," Akita responded.

"How...?" she muttered, glancing at Akita.

"You are not the only one good at disguising yourself," Akita said.

General Razdar Bahadur nodded to the security tech and stepped away. He watched on the screen as the Marastin Dow Edge military spacecraft entered the planet's orbit. He looked up when Zebulon, a Valdier warrior and head of security for Prince Mandra Reykill of the Valdier Royal family, stepped next to him.

"You are sure about your intel, Zebulon?" Razdar inquired.

Zebulon nodded. "The ship was on Kardosa and departed from the same sector as the killing. I had one of our inspectors place a tracking device on the ship. Footage from the vidcom identified the woman as Akita Maradash, General Reynar Maradash's sister and a known assassin that he employs. The dead man was a Triloug assassin named He'lo. The Docking Controller identified an injured woman as Captain Raia Glossman. She is human. Her body wasn't found, only her blood in the lift," he added.

Razdar nodded. "Do you have any idea why three assassins would be targeting a human freighter captain?" he asked.

Zebulon studied the screen. "There was a prison break on Spardonian. I'm sure you've been informed of the increased number of Marastin Dow warships outside of their normal space. There may be a connection. The Inspector said she was with a Tearnat business woman," he commented.

"Yes, I'm aware of the increase in the Marastin Dow forces. Has the Tearnat been interviewed?" Razdar asked.

Zebulon shook his head. "Strangely enough, the Tearnat has disappeared as well. She was last seen with some Chazen Desert Dwellers," he remarked.

Razdar lifted an eyebrow. "Kardosa is a strange place for Chazen Desert Dwellers. They normally do all their trading on their own planet," he reflected.

"Yes. What is especially interesting is that they arrived in a Tiliqua short hauler that later met up with a blacklisted Marastin Dow warship and docked in the lower level receiving bays. What are you going to do about Akita? She must have the human—assuming she is still alive. Why is she coming here knowing the risks, and where is she going?" Zebulon pondered.

Razdar's lips tightened when the ship on the screen veered to the northeast. "Notify flight control to prepare my personal transport," he ordered.

Zebulon looked at him with a startled expression. "Are you going after Akita? Wouldn't it make more sense to send in a ground team?" he suggested.

Razdar shook his head. "I don't want to catch Akita. I want to discover what she is up to. Do you want to come or not?" he asked.

Zebulon nodded. "By all means, I am intrigued now," he said.

Razdar glanced at the screen again before he turned and strode off the bridge of the sentry ship. He had been following Raia Glossman's journey ever since she met up with the Chazen on Yardell. There was only one place that Akita would risk going on Ceran-Pax. The question he wanted answered was which side was Raia Glossman and her adopted Marastin Dow family on—those trying to kill the Curizan Royal family or those trying to protect it?

Raia stumbled along the uneven ground when Akita pushed her. The woman had landed near the same group of trees that Raia had fourteen years ago. She didn't miss the irony of it. She had chosen the spot for its cover and location.

"You don't have to do this. My family knows nothing about what is going on. I told you I have no idea where Behr is. He felt the less information I knew, the safer it would be for me," she desperately shared.

"Quiet," Akita ordered, pushing between her shoulders again.

Raia twisted and raised her hands. She froze when Akita pressed the blaster barrel against her forehead. None of the moves Evetta and Hanine taught her over the years prepared her for a blaster between the eyes while wearing wrist cuffs.

"You might as well kill me now because I swear, I'll fight you until I draw my last breath before I let you harm my family," she hissed in a low voice.

"It is not your family I want," Akita said, lowering her weapon.

"He won't come. I told you, he has more important things to do than to save me. Do you really think that if he cared about me as much as you think he does, he would have left me?" she snapped.

"Yes, I do," Akita replied.

Raia frowned. There was that odd note in Akita's voice again. Akita motioned for her to turn and continue.

She pursed her lips, turned, and began walking again. They were just emerging from the path that opened up near the house when the rumble of a large spacecraft engine caused her to look up. She lifted her hands, shielding her eyes from the sunlight. She caught her breath when she saw the familiar markings of the *EA II*.

The noise from the freighter brought Evetta out of the house. Ben stepped out of the workshop with Bennie by his side. She stumbled to a stop when Akita reached out and wrapped her hand around her upper arm.

"He came," she unconsciously breathed out.

"As I knew he would," Akita murmured.

Behr rotated the freighter until the back platform was facing the house. He landed the freighter on the landing pad designed to pick up and deliver supplies. A quick visual as they were approaching showed the house and outer buildings. His attention was focused on the two women emerging from the tree line.

"I'll take out Akita as soon as you get Raia out of the way," Marus said.

"No," Behr replied.

Marus frowned. "What do you mean 'no'? She is too dangerous to leave alive," he stated.

"Let me… talk to her first," he said.

Marus scoffed. "You want to talk to an assassin? Have you completely lost your mind?" he demanded.

Behr powered down the freighter before he rose from his seat. He grimly smiled at the expression of incredulity on Marus's face. He looked down at the laser rifle lying next to the man.

"If you get a clear shot after Raia is out of danger, take it," he finally conceded.

"Thank you, Goddess, for a moment of sanity," Marus sarcastically retorted as he briefly looked up at the ceiling before glaring back at him.

"But only after I give you the signal," Behr added.

"*Trinorsis helo!*" 'Traitor's hell!' Marus cursed.

Behr ignored Marus's expletive and strode down the corridor to the loading bay. Chummy floated next to him while Pi popped ahead of them. He pressed the release on the platform and waited for the ramp to lower.

"You know what to do," he murmured.

We save Raia, Chummy said.

"Yes, we save Raia," he agreed with a deep sigh.

CHAPTER FIFTEEN

*R*aia's heart pounded so hard that she was sure Akita could hear it. The other woman had wrapped an arm around her neck and held a sharp blade to her throat. Raia kept her arms down in front and her eyes glued to the rear of the freighter.

"Behr," she whispered.

Akita's grip tightened, and Raia winced when the blade's sharp edge sliced a thin line along her skin. The woman eased the pressure but still kept the blade uncomfortably close. She stumbled when Akita nudged her forward.

Behr walked down the ramp and stopped at the end. He gazed at Raia, and the raw emotion she saw in his eyes took her breath away.

He loves me, she thought.

"Raia," Ben said, walking toward her.

"That is far enough," Akita stated.

Ben stopped ten feet away. Raia tried to give him a reassuring smile. Behind him, Bennie stood in the doorway, holding a rifle. Thankfully, he had it pointing toward the ground.

"We want no trouble. This is a peaceful place," Ben said.

"Peaceful?" Akita repeated.

Raia noticed Ben glancing in Bennie's direction. He waved his hand. Bennie knelt and lowered the rifle to the ground.

"Thank you," Raia muttered.

"Why?" Akita asked.

"Because you've never seen Bennie shoot. I have. He might be great on a video game, but in real life he couldn't hit a Pactor if it was standing ten feet in front of him," Raia answered.

"You are a strange, strange woman," Akita said, lowering the knife from her throat to her back.

Ben choked back a laugh. "Nice friends you have, Raia," he dryly commented.

"Well, you know how it is. There aren't that many female assassins in the universe, and I thought it might be nice to bring one home for you to meet," she quipped. Akita's grip tightened on her arm, and she winced. "Or maybe not."

"Are you two finished?" Akita demanded.

"Let her go, Akita. I'm the one you want," Behr ordered.

Raia trembled when Behr stepped up next to Ben. She couldn't help noticing that the two men were the same height and had similar builds. They were also dressed a lot alike.

It's strange the things that pass through one's mind when you have a knife to your throat, she mused.

"You are supposed to be off saving the star system, not me," she softly chided.

Behr's eyes darkened with emotion. "You were more important," he said. He turned his attention to Akita. "How do you want to do this?

I'll go peacefully with you if you promise not to hurt Raia and her family," he stated in a cool voice.

"No!" Raia hissed.

She no want to hurt. She come for help, Chummy's voice unexpectedly entered her thoughts.

"She what?" Raia mumbled, looking down.

Chummy was sitting on the ground next to Akita. He had one tiny paw pressed lightly against her leg. He stared up at Raia with wide eyes and wiggled his nose.

She was trying to process what Chummy was telling her when Pi suddenly appeared in front of Behr. The Peekaboo hit Behr in the chest as she materialized. A split second later, a blast flashed by them. Pi squealed with pain and dropped to the ground.

"Take cover!" Ben yelled.

Raia cried out when she saw the blood stain darkening Pi's coat. Behind her, Akita knocked her down to the ground next to the Peekaboo and twisted on one knee. Akita released a line of fire at the tree line.

"Get her out of here," Akita ordered, tossing the wrist cuff key to Behr.

Several more blasts exploded around them, kicking up bits of dust and rock. Raia scrambled over and scooped Pi into her arms. Behr grabbed the key out of the dust and wrapped his arm around her waist. Ben wrapped his arm around her other side, and the two men pulled her to her feet as Akita and someone from the freighter laid out some ground cover fire.

The three of them ran for the workshop. Bennie had picked up the rifle he laid on the ground earlier and was pointing it in the direction of the woods. Akita sprinted for cover behind a large field harvester.

"Let me take her," Evetta said, entering through the rear door and reaching for Pi as they passed through the doorway.

Raia held out her bound hands with Pi cupped between her palms. Behr turned her around and pressed the key against the wrist cuffs. They popped open and fell to the ground.

"Can I keep those?" Bennie asked.

"Give me the gun and go with your mother," Ben ordered with a shake of his head.

"Aw, Dad," Bennie complained.

"Bennie, you can help me with Pi," Evetta ordered.

"Get to the safe room," Ben instructed.

Evetta nodded. Bennie grumbled before he paled when a blast swept through the door and struck the shelf near his head. He hurried out the back after his mom with no more arguments.

"Where's Chummy?" Raia frantically asked, scanning the interior of the workshop.

"I don't know," Behr replied.

"I think I saw him with the woman," Ben said.

Raia crouched and tried to peer out the door. She fell back when an explosion rocked the building. Debris flew up, pelting her. Behr pulled her back against the wall.

"Go to the safe room," Behr said.

Raia wanted to protest, but deep down she knew there wasn't much she could do. She was good at sneaking into places and getting out. Behr, Ben, and Akita were more experienced in handling situations like this.

She gripped Behr's arm. "Find Chummy," she murmured.

"I will," he promised.

She braced her hand on the floor, preparing to sprint for the back door when Behr put his hand on her arm. She turned and looked at him. His eyes were dark and filled with a turbulent emotion. He pressed a hard kiss on her lips before he released her arm.

"I love you, Raia," he said.

A small smile curved her lips. "I know… oh, by the way, Chummy said Akita wasn't here to hurt us. She needs our help," she added before she sprinted for the back door as another explosion rocked the workshop.

~

"Here, this might work better," Ben said.

Behr reached out and caught the laser rifle Ben tossed to him. He checked it and noticed it had a full charge. He nodded his thanks to the man before he turned his attention outside.

"So, you love her," Ben asked.

Behr fired several shots through the open doorway before pulling back when there was return fire. "Yes," he replied.

"What are your intentions?" Ben asked, firing several shots before he was forced to take cover.

Behr looked at Ben. "Do you really want to have this conversation now?" he gritted out.

Ben looked over at him. "I might not get to have it if you or I get killed. What the hell is going on?" he asked.

Behr grimaced. "A Marastin Dow General named Maradash is working with a faction trying to kill the royal families of the Curizan, Valdier, and Sarafin so they can take over the star system," he said.

"What happened to a simple revolution to change your crazy social structure?" Ben asked.

"I'm working on that as well," Behr replied.

"So, who is trying to blow us to smithereens, and who is the woman that Raia says we now can't kill?" Ben grilled.

Behr fired several shots just as Akita and Marus fired. Whoever was trying to kill them sent a volley of fire in all three directions. Either there was more than one person, or the person was unbelievably fast.

"From the way they are attacking and the explosives used, I would say it is Orb, a Hoggian assassin hired by Maradash. He wants to kill Akita as much as he does me," he responded.

"And... who is Akita?" Ben probed.

"Maradash's sister," he said.

Ben looked at him in silence and shook his head. "We need to get out of here. We can go out the back. There is a drainage canal about two hundred yards away that will take us north of the woods. If your lady assassin and whoever the hell is in Raia's freighter can keep him busy, then we can take him by surprise," Ben suggested.

Behr shook his head. "He'll suspect we are on the move if there is no return fire from here. You stay here, shifting your fire from one side to the other. I'll go," he instructed.

Ben frowned. "Are you sure?" he asked.

"Yes," Behr replied.

Ben gave him a sharp nod of agreement and laid down a line of fire as Behr sprinted out the back door of the workshop. Behr crouched down and ran until he reached the drainage canal. Hopping over the side, he slid down the concrete retaining wall to the bottom. Fortunately, the water was only ankle deep. Heading north, he mentally calculated the distance he traveled based on the laser fire.

Ahead, he could see a set of iron steps embedded into the concrete. He shouldered the rifle, gripped the bars, and began climbing. He stopped near the top and peered over. He was slightly northwest of the trees where the laser fire was originating.

Climbing over the wall, he kept low as he worked his way across the field of tall grain. He passed through several rows until he was in line with the base of the woods. He slowed as he neared the tree line, calming his breathing, and focusing on the direction of the laser fire.

He slipped into the woods and cautiously stepped over fallen limbs. He scanned the area, the sight of his rifle level with his eyes. The scent of expelled laser fire grew stronger the farther he went.

A stray blast swept past him, and he pressed himself against the trunk of one of the thick trees. He would have to be careful. There was always the possibility that he might be hit by friendly fire.

He peered around the trunk. Twenty yards away, he saw movement. From the back, it looked like Orb was reloading a remote-controlled weapon. That was how he gave the impression of more than one shooter.

Orb's snarl mixed with the sound of laser fire. Through the stand of trees, Behr glimpsed Akita's white hair a split second before she fired. A stream of bright blue blood seeped from Orb's arm where she had grazed him.

That woman is deadly even when she can't see where her target is, he thought.

Using the distraction as cover, he advanced. He didn't want to shoot until he had a clear shot. A slight tug across his shin made him look down. A silent curse swept through his mind when he saw the tripwire. His gaze followed the wire to a weapon set up between two trees.

He backed up and stepped over the wire. He had to hand it to Orb for being prepared. It was obvious the assassin liked his weapons.

He scanned the area ahead. Laser blasts and explosions continued, but he lost sight of Orb. He took half a step forward when a sudden premonition of danger hit him. He twisted to his left just as Orb's beefy arm knocked his weapon from his hands, and it fell to the ground. Behr reeled and fell when Orb struck him in the jaw.

"About time you came out of hiding," Orb grunted, kicking the rifle into the brush.

Behr rubbed his jaw and climbed to his feet. He kept a wary eye on the assassin. He worked his jaw back and forth, thankful that it wasn't broken.

Orb slowly circled him, appearing unconcerned with the return fire coming from the farm. Orb lifted his hand and pressed a button. Seconds later, several explosions shook the ground. The Hoggian chuckled menacingly.

"Maradash isn't going to be happy with you if you kill Akita," he warned.

"Maradash is paying me another million credits to make sure that I do. He doesn't trust that bitch sister of his," Orb stated.

Behr frowned. "I'm surprised. He has a lot invested in her," he replied.

"He must have decided it was a bad investment. He doesn't want anyone more dangerous than he is running around—well, except for me," Orb chuckled.

"That's his mistake," Behr replied.

Orb's lips curled. "After I deal with you, I'll kill Akita and all the others except for your lady friend. Maradash wants you and her alive. He didn't say in what shape though. Maybe I'll leave you in one piece long enough to watch what I do to her. I'm going to start with cutting out her tongue," he said, pulling a blade from a sheath at his waist.

"It will never happen," Behr replied.

"Who's going to stop me… you?" Orb sneered.

"No. I think I'll let that pleasure go to a friend of mine," another voice commented.

He and Orb twisted at the same time to face their new threat. Behr blinked when he saw a man in a Curizan officer's uniform standing less than ten feet from them. The man was leaning against a tree, holding the weapon that Orb had set up as a booby-trap.

"You think you can stop me? A fancy Curizan officer," Orb snarled.

The Curizan chuckled and shook his head. "No, I prefer dealing with someone more challenging. My friend, though… he isn't as picky as I am," the man stated.

"And where is this friend hiding? Behind another tree?" Orb sneered.

"Actually, in one," the Curizan Officer announced, pointing upward.

Behr looked up along with Orb. He stumbled backward when the brilliant copper and black dragon perched on the limb above them released a burst of super-heated dragon fire. He lifted an arm, protecting his eyes from the bright blue flame. He was shocked that the concentration of the fire was focused on Orb and didn't extend more than a few inches around the man.

Orb's loud squeal faded almost as quickly as he uttered it. In seconds, only a pile of ash and two blackened broken tusks remain. Behr stared in stunned silence as the dragon dropped from the limb and shifted the moment his feet hit the ground.

"Someone more challenging, Bahadur?" the dragon-shifter dryly commented.

"I was merely distracting him for you, Zebulon," Razdar replied.

"Thank you," Behr said, looking at the two men.

"Don't thank us yet. There is still one more assassin that needs to be dealt with," Razdar stated.

Zebulon raised his hands. "I'll let you deal with Akita. She should be *challenging* enough for you. Personally, I don't care to kill women—unless they are trying to kill me first," he amended.

"If it is all the same to you, I'd like to be the one to deal with Akita," Behr said.

"She is a Marastin Dow assassin involved in an incident on Kardosa and was last seen holding a human hostage on Curizan protected land," Razdar pointed out.

"She isn't holding anyone hostage. Raia is safe. Akita… came to ask for assistance," he said, hoping that what Raia told him was correct.

"Assistance? Are we talking about the same person?" Zebulon asked with a skeptical expression.

"There are matters of grave concern that not only affect the Marastin Dow who want a new way of life but also the royal families of the Curizan, Valdier, and Sarafin. I've obtained information that may interest you…," he said.

"But…?" Razdar asked.

Behr looked at both men. "I want your promise that if I share the information, you'll allow us to leave. I believe you will understand why it would be in your interest to do so," he added.

"I'm General Razdar Bahadur. This is Zebulon, Chief of Security for Prince Mandra Reykill. We would both be interested in any information you may like to share," Razdar finally said.

"General Behr De'Mar," Behr said, holding out his hand. Razdar and Zebulon exchanged a surprised look. Behr grinned and nodded his head in the direction of the homestead. "Ben and Aaron told me this was a good way to show an alliance when I first met them many years ago."

Razdar slowly reached out and gripped Behr's hand, shaking it. "You wouldn't know a Marus Tylis, would you?" he asked.

Behr chuckled. "He is the one who was shooting from the freighter. Why do you ask?" he inquired.

"He saved the life of Prince Ha'ven's mate. That was when I suspected there must be something going on within the Marastin Dow," Razdar began.

Behr listened as they threaded their way through the woods. He called out a warning that they were coming out before they emerged from the woods into the clearing. Ben stepped out from the workshop while Akita cautiously rose from behind the harvester. Behr raised an eyebrow when he saw that she was cradling Chummy protectively in the crook of her arm. Marus slowly descended the freighter's ramp, his weapon at the ready and pointed at Akita.

"Stand down, Marus," he ordered.

Marus lowered his weapon to his side and warily watched as they approached. A cry of relief drew his attention, and he turned and saw Raia quickly descending the steps and running toward him. He caught her in his arms and hugged her close, ignoring their amused audience.

"We noticed on the security cams that the shooting had stopped," she said.

She leaned back and looked up at him. He winced when she touched his bruised cheek. Capturing her hand in his, he kissed her fingers.

"I'm fine. How is Pi?" he asked.

Tears filled Raia's eyes, and she shook her head. "It doesn't look good. Evetta isn't sure she will make it. The animal regenerator she has isn't programmed for the complex internal organs of a Peekaboo," she tearfully replied.

He held her tight when she buried her face against his shoulder as grief overwhelmed her. He stood still, caressing her back. Ben stepped forward and rubbed her shoulder in sympathy and understanding. They both understood how much Pi and Chummy meant to her.

Pressing his lips against her temple, he waited while she regained control. She drew in a shaky breath and sniffed. He gently wiped away a stray tear that coursed down her cheek.

"Let's go inside," he suggested.

Behr nodded. "There is a lot to discuss. Akita…," he called when the woman started to turn away. "I would like you to be there as well."

She looked at him and nodded. He wrapped his arm around Raia's waist, holding her close to his side. He owed a lot to Akita. The Marastin Dow assassin had saved Raia's life—just as he had saved Akita's over two decades before.

EPILOGUE

Spardonian Prison:
Marastin Dow Home World

Reynar turned away from the window where he was watching the reconstruction of the prison. The computer console chimed, alerting him to an incoming message. He walked over to the console and frowned when he noticed it was a video and not a live connection. He tapped to download the message.

On viewing the video, he pursed his lips into a firm line at the sight of two blackened, broken tusks on the screen before Akita's face filled the monitor. His hands fisted at the screen. He curled his fingers into a fist on witnessing the self-satisfied smirk on her face. She stared back at him with her glowing red eyes that sent a shiver down his spine.

"As you can see, brother, you have failed once again," she said in a voice dripping with acid. "Your mistake was in thinking you could kill me. You can't kill a ghost, Reynar. You already tried that once and it didn't work. I'm coming for you, Reynar. I'm coming for the Council. And I'm coming for the secret group you think will grant you unlimited power. There is nowhere you can hide that I can't find you. There is no assassin who can stop me. I was trained by the best, and your scientist made me better than any of them. I'll be in the shadows, and you won't even be aware that I'm there," she said. "I'll see you soon... *brother*."

Reynar punched the screen. His fist went through the hateful smirk on his sister's face, which reformed again when he pulled it back. He hated her. He had always hated her. That was why he tried to kill her.

"I'll be ready, *sister*," he vowed. "I'll be ready."

Ceran-Pax:

Behr rubbed Raia's shoulder. She lifted her head off the table where she had fallen asleep and looked up at him with blurry eyes. He encouraged her to stand, then swept her into his arms.

"Pi," she whispered, trying to look over his shoulder at the small Peek-aboo lying in the center of the medical bed.

"You get some sleep. I'll stay and watch over her," he promised.

Raia's eyes filled with tears. She turned her face into his neck and nodded. He carried her down the hallway to the bedroom that she used when she was visiting her friends. He gently lowered her to the bed and tucked the covers around her that he had turned down earlier.

"Try to get some sleep," he whispered, kissing her on the temple before he exited the room.

He quietly shut the door behind him and walked back down the hallway to the small medical room off the kitchen. He paused in the doorway. Akita stood by the bed, staring down at Pi.

"Akita," he greeted.

"You are getting sloppy. I heard you the moment you walked out of the bedroom," she reprimanded him.

He walked over and stood next to her. The anguish he felt increased when Chummy snuggled up next to Pi. The small Peekaboo's breathing was labored. Behr reached down and caressed her.

"Why does my chest hurt at the thought of this animal dying?" she asked.

"I don't know. Why do you think it does?" he asked.

"I'm not a good person," she finally said.

He shook his head. "You aren't a bad one either, Akita. I saw that and so did my father. You were forced to do bad things to survive," he said.

"No one is forced to do the things I've done unless they wanted to do them." She lifted her hand and studied it. "I see things that no one else can. All the horrors in minute detail."

He reached up and took her hand. "I think you could see the beauty in the universe the same way," he suggested.

"Why did you save my life all those years ago? You must have realized what my parents and brother were creating. Why would you save me?" she asked.

"Is that why you wanted to find me? So, that you could ask me?" he gently probed.

She stepped back from the bed. Chummy looked up at them before he rubbed his cheek against Pi and laid his head down again. Behr watched Akita turn and walk to the door.

"You want to know why I saved you, Akita? Because I thought you were worth saving. Yes, I knew what your parents and brother were creating, and I knew there was nothing I could do to stop them. You were your parents' most prized creation, but you were your brother's worst nightmare and that's what scares him the most," he said.

She paused at the door but didn't turn around. "Why... because they feared I would be just like they were... only deadlier?" she asked in a bitter tone.

"No. Because they feared you would be the opposite... only more powerful," he said.

She lifted her chin. "Your father and Ander Ray are still alive," she suddenly said in an unemotional tone.

"What...? That's impossible," he replied.

She shook her head and looked over her shoulder at him. "You do what you do best, Behr. I'll do what I do," she said.

"Akita...," he murmured.

She looked away from him. "We are on the same side now, Behr," she said before she walked out of the room.

Behr sank down into a chair. He was stunned. His father... and Ander Ray.... If it was true. He closed his eyes. He had given up hope years ago.

"Hope is a powerful emotion," a soft voice said.

He jerked upright at the unfamiliar voice. He gaped in stunned disbelief and rose from the chair, knocking it over in his haste. Standing across from him was a beautiful ethereal being made of gold.

"Who... who are you?" he hoarsely demanded.

"I am called Aminta," she replied.

She looked down at Chummy and Pi. Chummy sat up and raised one small paw up to her, as if begging for help. She brushed her hand over Chummy's head before she held her hand over Pi.

Behr was mesmerized by the flow of shimmering gold particles streaming from Aminta's palm and surrounding Pi. As if by magic, Pi's breathing grew steady and normal. She reminded him of the Valdier dragon's golden symbiots.

She smiled when Pi blinked and sat up. "Yes, I know you are hungry," she murmured.

Aminta waved her hand, and a bowl of fruit appeared. Behr studied the golden being with concern when her body shimmered and became translucent. She smiled at him.

"A small gift to help you in your fight," Aminta murmured before fading away.

Behr stood frozen in place for several minutes. He replayed the moment over and over in his mind. He looked at Pi and Chummy. They were now wrestling with each other on the table.

"How about we go wake Raia and let her know you are alright?" he suggested.

Then cookie and crème? Chummy asked with a hopeful expression.

Behr laughed. "Then you two can have all the cookies and crème you want," he promised.

Cookies! Chummy chortled with delight.

Pi had already disappeared. Behr was almost to the bedroom when he heard Raia's soft cry of happiness. His heart swelled with love on hearing her burst of happy sobs.

"Oh, Pi, I love you so much," she said.

NOTE FROM THE AUTHOR

I hope you enjoyed Behr's Rebel. I first introduced the Marastin Dow characters in Cornering Carmen. I loved the characters so much that I ended up writing A Warrior's Heart: Marastin Dow Book 1. Additional characters from their world appeared in Paul's Pursuit and Ha'ven's Song. The more I wrote more about the Marastin Dow, the more they came alive. Many of the characters in Behr's Rebel were in previous books. I look forward to writing more in this series and discovering the hidden Easter Eggs that link this world to many of my other stories and series. I hope you join me in the adventure.

Enjoy, Susan aka S.E. Smith

TO BE CONTINUED:

A genetically enhanced Marastin Dow assassin discovers love with the last man she expects… the father of the man who saved her life.

The Assassin's Quest: Marastin Dow Book 3

Akita studied the massive structure below her. It was heavily fortified, which came as no surprise. She scrutinized a land transport heading in her direction. She waited until it was level with her position on the rock plateau.

Rising to her feet, she ran along the edge and jumped. When she landed on the transport, she rolled and came up on one knee, crouching low as it swept past the gates leading into the structure.

ADDITIONAL BOOKS

If you loved this story by me (S.E. Smith) please leave a review! You can discover additional books at: http://sesmithfl.com and http://sesmithya.com or find your favorite way to keep in touch here: https://sesmithfl.com/contact-me/ Be sure to sign up for my newsletter to hear about new releases!

Recommended Reading Order Lists:

http://sesmithfl.com/reading-list-by-events/

http://sesmithfl.com/reading-list-by-series/

The Series

Science Fiction / Romance

Dragon Lords of Valdier Series

It all started with a king who crashed on Earth, desperately hurt. He inadvertently discovered a species that would save his own.

Curizan Warrior Series

The Curizans have a secret, kept even from their closest allies, but even they are not immune to the draw of a little known species from an isolated planet called Earth.

Marastin Dow Warriors Series

The Marastin Dow are reviled and feared for their ruthlessness, but not all want to live a life of murder. Some wait for just the right time to escape...or change everything.

Sarafin Warriors Series

A hilariously ridiculous human family who happen to be quite formidable... and a secret hidden on Earth. The origin of the Sarafin species is more than it seems. Those cat-shifting aliens won't know what hit them!

Dragonlings of Valdier Novellas

The Valdier, Sarafin, and Curizan Lords had children who just cannot stop getting into trouble! There is nothing as cute or funny as magical, shapeshifting kids, and nothing as heartwarming as family.

Cosmos' Gateway Series

Cosmos created a portal between his lab and the warriors of Prime. Discover new worlds, new species, and outrageous adventures as secrets are unravelled and bridges are crossed.

The Alliance Series

When Earth received its first visitors from space, the planet was thrown into a panicked chaos. The Trivators came to bring Earth into the Alliance of Star Systems, but now they must take control to prevent the humans from destroying themselves. No one was prepared for how the humans will affect the Trivators, though, starting with a family of three sisters….

Lords of Kassis Series

It began with a random abduction and a stowaway, and yet, somehow, the Kassisans knew the humans were coming long before now. The fate of more than one world hangs in the balance, and time is not always linear….

Zion Warriors Series

Time travel, epic heroics, and love beyond measure. Sci-fi adventures with heart and soul, laughter, and awe-inspiring discovery…

Paranormal / Fantasy / Romance

Magic, New Mexico Series

Within New Mexico is a small town named Magic, an… unusual town, to say the least. With no beginning and no end, spanning genres, authors, and universes, hilarity and drama combine to keep you on the edge of your seat!

Spirit Pass Series

There is a physical connection between two times. Follow the stories of those who travel back and forth. These westerns are as wild as they come!

Second Chance Series

Stand-alone worlds featuring a woman who remembers her own death. Fiery and mysterious, these books will steal your heart.

More Than Human Series

Long ago there was a war on Earth between shifters and humans. Humans lost, and today they know they will become extinct if something is not done....

The Fairy Tale Series

A twist on your favorite fairy tales!

A Seven Kingdoms Tale

Long ago, a strange entity came to the Seven Kingdoms to conquer and feed on their life force. It found a host, and she battled it within her body for centuries while destruction and devastation surrounded her. Our story begins when the end is near, and a portal is opened....

Epic Science Fiction / Action Adventure

Project Gliese 581G Series

An international team leave Earth to investigate a mysterious object in our solar system that was clearly made by someone, someone who isn't from Earth. Discover new worlds and conflicts in a sci-fi adventure sure to become your favorite!

New Adult / Young Adult

Breaking Free Series

A journey that will challenge everything she has ever believed about herself as danger reveals itself in sudden, heart-stopping moments.

The Dust Series

Fragments of a comet hit Earth, and Dust wakes to discover the world as he knew it is gone. It isn't the only thing that has changed, though, so has Dust...

ABOUT THE AUTHOR

S.E. Smith is an *internationally acclaimed, New York Times* **and** *USA TODAY Bestselling* author of science fiction, romance, fantasy, paranormal, and contemporary works for adults, young adults, and children. She enjoys writing a wide variety of genres that pull her readers into worlds that take them away.

Made in United States
Orlando, FL
11 February 2022

14742152R00124